The doctors were sure his memory would not return.

Danielle didn't know how it could possibly be that she was a stranger to the man she'd loved so fiercely, who'd been her best friend and husband for more than seven years and the father of their two children. She hadn't realized how much she had hoped the sight of their house would spark something for him.

There was no recognition in his eyes as he turned to her. "We live here?"

"We moved in right before Tyler was born."

"Tyler." Sad lines crinkled around Jonas's eyes. "I wish I could remember my own kids."

Tyler pounded into the room just then, threw his arms wide and wrapped them around Jonas. "Daddy, you're home!"

Jonas's eyes filled with emotion as he ran an awkward hand over the top of his little son's head, affectionate and sweet and devoted.

What truly mattered *hadn't* changed.

Books by Jillian Hart

Love Inspired

*The McKaslin Clan
**A Tiny Blessings Tale

Love Inspired Historical

JILLIAN HART

makes her home in Washington State, where she has lived most of her life. When Jillian is not hard at work on her next story, she loves to read, go to lunch with her friends and spend quiet evenings with her family.

Her Wedding Wish
Jillian Hart

Steeple Hill®

Published by Steeple Hill Books™

STEEPLE HILL BOOKS

Steeple
Hill®

ISBN-13: 978-0-373-87483-5
ISBN-10:   0-373-87483-9

HER WEDDING WISH

Copyright © 2008 by Jill Strickler

www.SteepleHill.com

Printed in U.S.A.

See, I am sending an angel ahead of you
to guard you along the way and to bring you
to the place I have prepared.

—Exodus 23:20

Prologue

Danielle Lowell had never felt so cold as she followed the desk nurse along the dimly lit, tomblike corridors of the hospital. Their movements echoed along the barren walls like heartbeats—first the muted pad of the nurse's rubber-soled shoes, and then the tap, tap of her open-toed sandals.

When she looked down, she saw, in contrast to the scuffed beige floor tiles, the cheerful cotton-candy pink of her toenails. She had painted them just this morning, both hers and her daughter's while holding the toddler on her lap. Madison had giggled and babbled with glee. Danielle had been happy, as warm as the cheerful June sunshine.

Now, hours later, it was as if the sun had gone down forever. Her veins had turned to ice, her heart to a glacier.

An eternity had passed since that afternoon when she'd answered her cell phone to the sound of Jonas's supervisor's voice. She'd known it was bad news even before Rick had said the words. She'd felt a warm embrace, as if comforting arms had wrapped around her chest, as if someone was holding her tightly.

At the back of her mind she wondered if her husband was dead and she felt his spirit, his soul, somehow come to tell her goodbye. But the touch didn't feel familiar, and maybe it was the effect of too much sun.

Either way, she knew the words before Rick spoke them. *Jonas has been shot in the line of duty.*

"You have ten minutes." The nurse's voice startled her, although she spoke in a modulated, almost whisper. "Your husband is unconscious, so don't be alarmed. The equipment can look frightening at first. Hold his hand. Talk to him. He'll hear you."

"How can that be? They told me he's in a coma. Has he woken up?" That faint hope flickered like a new flame in a harsh wind and died.

"No, he's in a deep coma, I'm afraid. That hasn't changed. But studies have taught us that hearing is the last of the senses to fail. Besides, I believe our hearts are always listening. His will know yours. God bless." She led the way into the small isolated room.

Danielle stumbled at the sight of the stranger on the bed, waxy looking and motionless. *Jonas.* Her heart cracked and, like the edge of a glacier, sheared off.

This was her husband? Her knees failed and she hit the ground, kneeling at his side. The beep of the monitors, the ticking that marked his heart, the whir of a ventilator were out of a nightmare. She stared at the bags of fluid and drugs that hung like Japanese lanterns around his bedside. Shock took what little life was left in her.

My poor Jonas. His face was different—two already bruising black eyes, a stitched gash over his cheekbone and his hair shaved to his bare scalp, marred by a zigzagged suture line and bandages.

He looked already gone, despite the rise and fall of his chest.

Lord, don't let him go. It was a plea that tore up from her soul. Without words, she gathered Jonas's cool hand carefully in hers. It didn't feel like his hand, which had always been so big and capable, and was now feeble and still.

"Don't leave me, Jonas." Fear shattered her. Choking on grief, she leaned her forehead against the palm of his cool hand.

What had occupied her thoughts earlier in the day—balancing their monthly budget and their minor disagreement this morning and the overgrown hedges needing clipping—slipped away. Nothing mattered but her husband and his life.

Please, Lord, don't take him, she prayed, but she heard no answer above the noise of the machines. So she held on to him tight, as if she had the impossible strength to hold his soul to his body.

She felt arms wrap like comfort around her again, but she saw no one and nothing in the translucent light. Jonas's pulse slowed a beat, as if his heart became aware of hers through the void.

Chapter One

One year later

Danielle slowed the minivan and turned into the driveway. As she eased her foot onto the brake she turned her attention to Jonas in the front passenger seat, a stranger to her now after his coma and brain injury. She wished she could control the quake of her pulse as she watched his face, his dear, handsome face. His forehead furrowed in thought as he studied the house in front of them—the home they'd fallen in love with together.

Oh, Lord, let him remember. It was a lot to ask, she knew. From the moment he'd woken from a deep coma and through a long stay at an intensive rehabilitation clinic in Seattle, he hadn't had a single recollection of their lives together. All the memories they'd made together were lost to him. And without those memories, he looked at her with a stranger's gaze. The doctors had been very sure his memory would not return.

She didn't know how it could be that she was a stranger to the man she'd loved so fiercely, who'd been her best friend and husband for over seven years and the father of their two children. She didn't realize how much she had hoped the sight of their house would spark something for him.

No recognition flared in his eyes as he turned to her. "We live here?"

"Yes." The word scratched like sandpaper against the inside of her throat. She tried hard not to let her disappointment show as she hit the remote on the visor. The garage door opened. "We had the house built and we moved in right before Tyler was born."

"Tyler." Sad lines crinkled around Jonas's eyes. "Is he waiting?"

"He's not home right now."

"Yes, that's right." He released a heartfelt sigh and rubbed his forehead as if it were hurting him. He looked truly distressed, but maybe the worst pain wasn't physical. "I wish I could remember my own kids."

"Me, too." She eased the minivan into the garage. "My sister Katherine will be bringing them home in a little while. She was thoughtful enough to offer to take them a bit longer, so you could face things one step at a time."

"Katherine is the one in college?"

"No, that's Rebecca. Katherine is my older sister."

"Oh. Okay." He gave a wobbly half smile, half frown. The left side of his face still troubled him. "I *will* get it."

"You will. Don't worry."

She pulled the emergency brake and shut off the engine, deliberately concentrating on each task because it was predictable and familiar. Unlike her marriage. She'd been praying for this day to come for so long, it had begun to feel unreal and impossible.

Now, after a long hospital stay and a longer period in rehabilitation, they were alone together. The garage door slid shut behind them. She was alone with her husband, the man she no longer knew. The man who could not remember the simplest things about their marriage. When he turned his questioning gaze to hers, she knew that he did not know what to expect. He remembered nothing new.

Disappointment sifted through her. She didn't realize she was holding her breath until she felt her lungs burn. She had to remember to breathe. She had faith, and it would lift them both up, right?

Right, she told herself, fighting off a world of doubt, despite her strong belief. The journey ahead of her—of them—seemed monumental.

"Let's go inside, and maybe once you're in the house things will seem more familiar to you." She grabbed her keys and her purse and forced a smile.

His dear face, the same in many ways and changed in others, stared back at her. "What if it doesn't? I'm—" He grimaced. "I don't know the word. I'm—" Frustrated, he stared down at his gnarled hand.

"It doesn't matter, Jonas. It's okay." She wanted to believe that.

As she stepped from the seat and closed the door behind her, she realized he was still sitting in the minivan, with tension on his face and sadness in his eyes. What must it be like, she wondered, to come home to a place you could not remember? To feel the weight of a wife's need and expectations?

She took another deep breath and opened his car door. Poor Jonas. She helped him out and unfolded his walker. His right hand gripped the walker's handles with white-knuckled force while his left one struggled to do so. All the love in her heart flooded out, filling her with sweet tenderness. This was hard for her, but it was harder for him, and at least he was here. He was *here*. She was deeply grateful for that.

She slipped her purse strap onto her shoulder and her keys into her jacket pocket and took Jonas's frail arm. "This is going to be tricky. It's a long way to the door for you, so lean on me."

"I can get it." He looked so determined as he moved his nerve-damaged leg.

While the Good Lord had been gracious in bringing Jonas back to her, the bullet had not been kind. Her heart broke as he struggled so hard to cross the garage floor, even with her help. By the quiet steely set to his jaw, she could tell he hated it. Her once-strong, invincible husband, who rarely missed a workout at the gym the entire time she'd known him, was now forced to lean on her and his walker.

"Don't tell me," he quipped between struggled steps. "I used to do this faster."

"Yes, you did." Danielle unlocked the garage door. "But I always said our lives were going by too fast, we were always rushing here and there. It's nice to slow down and take in the sights."

He stopped to smile, and his grin was lopsided and strained. "I'm taking the, what is it, slow—something?"

"It's the scenic route." She hit the remote on her key ring and the security system stopped beeping. She held the door patiently while he struggled to get his walker and then his feet over the doorstep. She stopped him with a touch of her hand to his. "Look around. You made it. You're home."

He was silent for a moment, gazing down the hall as if taking in the details of woodwork and walls, of the living room ahead and, to the right, the archway leading to the kitchen. "The kids."

At first she didn't know what he meant, but then she realized he was commenting on the framed photographs marching along the wall. "Yes. These are the pictures I have taken once a year at a professional photographer."

"That's why they're tidy."

"Yes." She looked at the carefully posed photographs with rich backgrounds. "The kids are in their best clothes. It was a challenge keeping them that clean and neat for the short drive from here to their appointments."

"No ice cream in the car?" There was that lopsided grin again, but this time with a hint of his old smile, too.

Her heart filled at the glimpse of her husband she knew and loved so well. "No ice cream," she agreed. "They had to wait until after the sitting. I have more pictures throughout the house, but they're snapshots."

"Not as tidy."

"No. In fact, there are some very messy pictures."

"Pictures of you, too?" His smile faded. Something serious, and maybe a little bit fearful, came onto his face.

I wish I knew what he was feeling, she thought wistfully. Once, she'd known him so well, there would have been no question. She would have known what he was thinking even before he did.

Determined to stay upbeat, she laid her hand on his broad shoulder. "Yes, there are pictures of me. And of you."

"I want to see them."

"Sure, but it's going to take a long time to go through them. There are so many."

"I've got time. Lots of time."

She watched the pain on his face and didn't know what more to say. "Down the hall is the living room. Let's get you sitting down."

"I need to rest." He nodded once in agreement and set his chin. After gripping the handles of his walker tightly, he concentrated on stepping forward. The carpet absorbed most of the thunk and shuffling sounds as he painfully made his way down the short hallway. He was out of breath by the time he reached the living room. She supported his elbow as he dropped, exhausted, onto the couch.

"I'll be right back." She smiled at him.

There wasn't the zing of emotional connection that had always been between them, and as she hurried to the kitchen, she fought deeper frustrations. Why had she thought things would be better once they were home?

It wasn't fair to put so much pressure on him, she realized while she filled his favorite mug with water and zapped it in the microwave.

She needed to give him all the time he needed, no matter how hard that would be. He'd asked for pictures, and that's where they would start. As the water heated, she grabbed a small book of snapshots from the corner hutch in the dining room. She caught her husband watching her as she came toward him.

He looked terribly serious, and she wondered if he was disappointed in her. She was painfully aware of the wash-worn jeans she'd put on this morning—the laundry was woefully behind—and the favorite summery T-shirt was hardly high fashion.

She'd been spending so little thought and even less time on her appearance. What if she looked like Frankenstein's bride after standing all night in the rain? Worse, when was the last time she'd glanced in a mirror? Who knew what her hair was doing? And what about the big dark bags under her eyes from long-term sleep deprivation?

No wonder he was looking a little panicked. She slid the small book onto the coffee table that separated them. "These were the pictures we took on our last vacation. Maybe that will be a good place to start."

"Vacation." He stretched out his hand, straightening his fingers, and snagged the book from the table. "Where'd we go?"

"I'm not telling. See if you can figure it out."

"Someplace important, then." He watched her carefully, and his emotion was unreadable to her. "I'll see what I can do."

The bing of the microwave saved her. "I'll be right back."

She spun on the heel of her sneakers and retreated to the safety of the kitchen. This was worse than starting out on a first date with someone, she thought as she rescued the steaming mug. Back then, she'd felt comfortable with Jonas right from the start, so their first date had been familiar, as if meant to be.

But this, now with him, was painful in too many ways to count. She plucked a bag from a tea box and dropped it into the water to steep. In the next room, she could hear the slight creak of the photo album's binding and the first squeaking turn of the plastic-coated pages.

She'd spent hours on that book—before Jonas's accident she'd been a serious scrapbooking fanatic. It had been the last project she'd finished before he'd been shot. She didn't dare think about the others in progress stuffed in the back of her downstairs craft closet. Yikes. Considering the importance of those pictures now, maybe she should find the time to finish them.

After dunking and squeezing the tea bag, she added a teaspoon of honey. It was silent in the living room, so she peered around the kitchen corner just enough to see him on the couch. Jonas, her husband, looked different from the man he'd been—his hair was too short, his big physical frame no longer imposing or strong. Yet there was much that had remained the same—that tensile, decent goodness of his that she loved so much.

Her heart filled, watching as he studied the first page. His face lined with concentration, he lifted his right hand—he used to be left-handed—and ran his finger across the plastic-sheathed page. Emotion welled in his eyes, and she felt it like a bolt of lightning. Stricken, she pulled back into the kitchen, longing, just longing for everything to be all right. For the pieces of their lives to be put back in place.

She hurried about, putting his favorite chocolate cookies on a plate. By the time she'd loaded everything on a small tray and carried it into the living room, Jonas had leaned back onto the couch and had the book open on his knees.

He looked up with a grin on his face. "That sure smells good."

"I hope so." She slid the plate onto the coffee table first and then handed him a soft cookie.

He paused before he took a bite. "I liked the ones you sent in the box."

When he'd been in rehabilitation, she'd sent weekly care packages, when she hadn't been able to make the long trip to Seattle. "The oatmeal-raisin cookies didn't break when I shipped them," she explained as she eased beside him onto the couch. "I was saving these for a homecoming surprise."

He took a bite. "Good. Very good. I like them."

She knew he wouldn't remember they were his favorite, or that she'd made them all the time for him when they'd been dating. That he'd said—oh, her heart cracked deeply remembering—

"I can see why I married you." He held up the remaining half of the cookie. "Why? What did I say?"

The room suddenly blurred, and she shook her head, blinking hard. She reached for a cookie. "That's what you used to say before you proposed to me."

"Yeah? What else can you make? Maybe I'll have to propose again."

There was that ghost of his grin. How good it was to see. She relaxed against the cushions. "You'll have to wait and see. What do you think of the pictures?"

"I sure got a pretty wife."

"Now you're just trying to get more cookies."

"Sure, but it's true." He took another cookie from the plate with his awkward fingers. "I'm a lucky man." He tapped the page with his knuckle. "What's that?"

"Mom and Dad's RV. It's a motor home." When he stared at her uncomprehendingly, she explained, "You drive it and sleep in it."

"We did?"

"Handsome, you drove that monster." She didn't suppose he remembered their half affectionate and half not-so-affectionate name for the vehicle that had been hard to park and harder to maneuver along narrow roads. She leaned close to get a better look at the page.

The digital pictures, which she'd printed off on the snazzy little photo printer her twin sisters had given her for her last birthday, showed them starting out from their driveway. She looked at herself and groaned. Even with Madison on her hip, her tummy problem still showed. Goodness. She sighed. Otherwise, the snapshot looked great. Tyler was grinning wide, practically a blur of motion. "It had been almost impossible for Tyler to stand still for a single moment. He was so excited that morning."

"He looks happy." Jonas swallowed, as if he were struggling with emotions. "Everybody did."

"It was your first vacation all year." Somehow, remembering made her heart warm, made the distance between her and this new, different Jonas less cumbersome. "You got everyone up early, you were so excited to go, and made everyone breakfast before we left. It was wonderful, and a little easier on me."

"You make breakfast?"

"Just about every morning." She didn't add how, that long-ago morning, he'd hugged her so tightly and sweetly and whispered in her ear how glad he was to be able to spend the next two weeks with her. Then he'd set the timer on the camera and rushed back to the steps to scoot in next to her, and tickle Tyler so he was laughing when the timer went off.

Maybe he would remember that in time, she hoped. "Turn the page and you'll see—"

She waited while he fumbled with the thick plastic edge. She hated how hard he had to work to turn the page and she waited, not knowing if it would hurt his pride worse to have her help, but he finally managed it on his own. His strong beautiful hand was slightly bent and twisted, a condition that the neurologists thought would gradually disappear. She resisted the urge to take his fingers in hers and massage them, as if she could rub that partial paralysis away.

"I'm driving." He looked surprised. "I had hair."

"Yes, and it will grow back."

He looked sheepish and nodded. He studied the page for a long time. They were the photos she'd taken from the front passenger seat of Jonas driving away from their home, of Tyler wearing his fireman hat and strapped into his seat, grinning ear to ear, and of Madison yawning hugely in her car seat. Her soft brown curls were like a cloud around her button face. Danielle felt full to the brim. Her family. Her loves. Her everything.

When Jonas turned to the facing page, his lopsided smile widened. Happiness lit his eyes. He tapped the page where they'd pulled over to the side of a small-town street. In the cluster of small pictures, Jonas was holding his son's hand, so small in his big capable one, and they stood side by side watching a hawk perched on a high branch of a tree. Another picture showed Tyler's little face staring trustingly up at his father—so vulnerable and good and sweet.

Jonas swallowed visibly. "I don't want to—" He stopped, as if searching for the word. "I don't want to—" He shook his head. Lines of frustration and misery dug into his handsome face. "I can't think of the word."

She laid her hand on his and felt the warm unyielding band

of his wedding ring beneath her palm. "I'm glad to have you home, Jonas. If you're worried about disappointing us—"

He nodded. "That's the word. I—" He shrugged helplessly, unable to say what was in his heart.

But she knew. Even as injured as he was, she would always know her husband's heart. "You're here. That means more than you know. The rest of it—the remembering, everything—it will get easier."

Relief passed across his face and he nodded once, his gaze fastened on hers. She hadn't realized how much he needed this, too, to be here, to try to find their normal lives again. She watched as he touched the snapshot with Tyler gazing up adoringly, full of awe and love for his dad. Jonas cleared his throat. "I don't want to disappoint."

"Tyler just wants you to love him. It will be all right."

He nodded and looked away, unreadable, like a stranger once more.

Danielle took a shaky breath and removed her hand. She waited as he turned to the next page, studying the picnic they'd had at a small park along the way, taking in the sunshine beneath the awning of the RV, laughing and sunny. She hadn't realized how perfect their lives had been at that moment, with Madison messy and fussy and Tyler hyper from being buckled in for the morning, and the weight of worry and responsibility nagging at her. She would give nearly anything to have her husband look at her now the way he did in the photo, as if he knew her better than she knew herself and loved her, every shortcoming, every flaw, every strength.

"This is a good book." Jonas tapped the picture he'd taken—and didn't remember—of her buckling in Madison, who was in the middle of struggling, chubby arms reaching toward her daddy. "I can see a lot."

She was glad she'd taken the time to make the album, the careful cutting and pasting, the rubber-stamping and gluing and framing, the glitter and cutouts and ribbons. These memories and pictures were more important now than ever. She'd originally started the books so that they wouldn't forget the good times and the small details about the kids—they were growing so fast!—but now it had a larger purpose. To remember where they'd been. For what could be again.

The front door opened, and the security system chimed an announcement.

"Hello?" Her older sister Katherine's voice echoed in the foyer over the sound of running little-boy feet. "Anybody home?"

For a nanosecond, Jonas's gaze found hers, the panic raw and honest on his face. So many expectations, because Tyler didn't know his daddy couldn't remember him. They had decided together that it wouldn't be right to hurt him that way, to rock his security like that. So, the little boy who pounded into the room, his brown hair sticking straight up, only knew his daddy had been hurt and was now home to stay. Excitement lit him up like a lightbulb as he threw his arms wide and wrapped them around Jonas.

"You're here! Daddy, you're home!" Tyler didn't let go but laid his cheek on his dad's wide chest and grinned up at him. "Aunt Katherine brought nachos and Mexi-fries just for you."

Danielle knew that the man beside her no longer knew the significance of their inside joke of Mexi-fries, but that didn't matter. Jonas's eyes filled with emotion as he ran an awkward hand over the top of his little son's head, affectionate and sweet and devoted.

What truly mattered hadn't changed.

Chapter Two

Danielle walked into the kitchen and saw her sister. Katherine had Madison on her hip and was unloading two bags of food from their favorite Mexican take-out restaurant.

"Mommy!" Madison's arms shot out and she thrust herself through the air, trusting her aunt had a solid hold on her.

Danielle came to her rescue as Katherine held the half-prone princess. Her little play tiara was askew, sitting crooked in those soft light brown curls, and Madison was bright with happiness. Danielle wrapped a secure arm around her daughter and hefted her onto her hip.

"They've both been wound up all day." With her sleek blond locks, girl-next-door loveliness and great clothes sense, Katherine was cover-model gorgeous, even four months pregnant. She reached out to straighten Madison's tiara. "Jonas is in the living room?"

"Yes, Tyler is with him. He's been waiting a long time for his daddy to come home, poor baby." She set Madison to the floor and the little girl immediately spun around and stretched both hands toward the out-of-reach counter.

"Gotta get my phone!" she singsonged, while her aunt produced the plastic pink cell phone from the collection of stuff on the counter. "There you go, sweetie. Dani, you look tired. Are you feeling a little worse for wear?"

"And a little short of time. Know where I can buy a few more hours to add to the day?"

"I wish I did, believe me. I'd be the first one in line." Katherine wrapped her in a hug. "You've been going hard all day, which is what I figured. That's why I brought dinner. It's a little earlier than your normal suppertime, but I thought you'd be too tired to fix a meal."

"Could you be more wonderful?" Danielle thought of all that her sister had done for her, and not only Katherine, but her entire family—her brother and sisters and her parents, not to mention her church family. "Like you don't have enough to do?"

"My Jack wasn't hurt in the line of duty."

"Thank God for that." Danielle prayed for her brother-in-law every day. Katherine's husband was also a state trooper; Jonas had helped his childhood friend Jack get his job when he moved to Montana last year.

Such violence, like the kind that touched their family, wasn't common in this part of Montana, but no place was immune, it seemed. The silver lining in this dark time was seeing for sure there was much more good in the world—in people—than bad. "Kath, thanks for taking the kids and for thinking to pick up dinner. For everything."

"No problem. I wish I would have had the time to make you a real dinner, but there's a youth group basketball game tonight. Jack stayed behind to help Hayden get ready."

Danielle adored her sister's stepdaughter. Hayden was

thriving, active in their church and excelling at school, which was done for the summer. "She's starting tonight?"

"Talk about excited. She's worked so hard. I know she's going to do well tonight as a starter."

"Then you don't want to miss the tip-off. You'd better be going." Danielle laid her hand gently on her little princess's small shoulder. Madison, chatting away, grinned up at her and kept prattling. "What time's the game?"

"Not to worry." Katherine swirled to the sink and turned on the tap. "I've got a little bit of time before I have to leave. I might as well make myself useful here. Why don't you take your little one in to see her daddy, sit down and spend time with your family? Your whole family. Together."

"I know. It's almost unbelievable. I've been praying for this for so long, I can't believe it's finally here."

"It puts a different meaning to the word blessings, doesn't it?"

The four of them together in the same house. Danielle's throat ached with gratitude. How very easily this moment could have never happened.

Katherine washed her hands and reached for a towel. "Oh, I can hear Tyler."

They both strained to listen to the little boy in the neighboring room, his voice clear and sweet. "Daddy, that's the picture where you hit your knee when you was climbin' up the steps, and you hopped around. Your whole foot tingled so Mom had to drive until we saw the moose."

"You remember all that?" Jonas asked in his resonant baritone.

"Yep. I remember lotza stuff. I got lotza brains."

Danielle put her hand over her mouth to hold in the giggle.

"Go on." Katherine's eyes were sparkling with mirth as she dried her hands. "Get back to your husband. I've got it covered here."

"I owe you. Expect retaliation when you least expect it."

"Oh, that would be wonderful. You know how I love your lasagna."

"I know." One evening soon, she'd make sure to pay back Katherine for her thoughtfulness tonight, but it couldn't be enough. Nothing could be. It had been twelve long months that her entire family had been rallying around her and pitching in with the housework and the child care. As much as she appreciated it—and she did very much— the weight of the guilt over inconveniencing them choked her. It was time to start paying back.

She put her hand on her daughter's soft downy head and gently turned her in the direction of the living room. They went a few paces before Madison suddenly stopped chatting, wrapped one arm around Danielle's knee and dug in her heels.

Strange. Danielle knew that the little girl hadn't seen Jonas since their brief trip to Seattle for Christmas. "C'mon, baby, let's go see your daddy."

"No." Madison dropped her phone and buried her face in her hands.

Danielle knelt down—which was awkward since Madison still had one arm tightly around her knee—and realized Jonas was watching them from the couch. Tyler was camped down beside his dad on the cushion, his feet tucked beneath him, shoes and all.

"C'mon, Madison!" Tyler called out. "Mom made the fudge cookies."

"Fudge cookies?" Madison spread two chubby fingers to peer out and verify the truth of her big brother's claim.

And right before supper, too, Danielle thought. "Only one, both of you, or you'll spoil your dinner."

It was tough being the mom, because she had to face Tyler's groan and Madison's gasp of distress at such news. She gently nudged her daughter forward a step. "Go on, sweetie. Tyler has a cookie for you."

"No." Madison removed one hand from her face, held up two fingers, reconsidered, and held up three, which meant she wanted three cookies. Her adorable little chin jutted.

Danielle knew that look. Ah, the terrible twos were such a joy. She took a breath and gathered her courage for the impending battle—knowing she'd come out unpopular in the end—and then she felt Katherine's hand on her shoulder.

"She reminds me of someone," Katherine said innocently. "Who could it be?"

"Not me." Danielle started to laugh, even as she denied it. "I'm not stubborn and never have been."

"No, not you," Katherine agreed, laughing, as she opened the refrigerator door.

Yep, her mother had warned her this day would come. She figured the best way to deal with having a daughter just like herself was to embrace it. She unwrapped Madison from her knee. "It's too bad you don't want a cookie."

"No! No! Bring me some!"

Danielle sighed and turned her back, unable to ignore the fact that her sister was silently laughing as she gathered condiments from the refrigerator.

"Just you wait," she told Katherine as Madison's outrage was about to start. "This is what babies turn into."

Not that she minded, but Madison could really scream—a sound best avoided. "I'm going to have to invest in some earplugs."

"Or something." Katherine was still laughing.

"Hi there, Madison," came Jonas's deep and gentle voice from across the room. "You want a cookie?"

Danielle turned to see their daughter's reaction. Madison's face, red with the beginnings of a typical two-year-old tantrum, scrunched with thought. Her chin stayed up a notch, and slowly she shook her head side to side.

"No!" Madison uttered that word with impressive force. She held up four fingers.

"Suit yourself," Jonas said, good-naturedly. "Tyler and I will eat 'em."

Madison's jaw dropped in surprise. She'd been startled out of her tantrum.

As Danielle knelt to retrieve Madison's plastic pink phone, Jonas's gaze fastened on hers. She smiled a thank-you to him, and he nodded in acknowledgment. By the time she'd handed Madison her play cell, Jonas had gone back to studying the album.

His steady baritone was warm with kindness as he asked their son, "What's this here?"

Tyler, brimming with happiness, pointed to the picture. "That's where we got to make a campfire. And we had to make sure we had buckets of water and dirt ready in case it went out of control, so we didn't start a forest fire."

"You did a good job."

"Yep, I did. I made sure there was no forest fires! Then, after we did the s'mores—"

"Mores?" Jonas asked, and was rewarded with Tyler's

explanation of the huge s'mores they'd made together, the biggest ones in the whole world.

Danielle heard Katherine behind her.

"It's going well," Katherine whispered, and there was a smile in her voice as she padded by on the way to the dining room table.

It *was* going well. She took one last look at her husband and son, side by side on the couch, already buddies again. No matter what they'd lost, and with the remaining challenges of Jonas's injuries still standing between them, they had a little bit of their normal family life back.

Lord, this means everything. Thank You.

Danielle straightened Madison's pink rhinestone tiara before she opened the closest cabinet door and counted out enough plates for everyone. Madison stood in place, watching her father with wide staring eyes.

"Want to go in and see your daddy, sweetie?"

She shook her head, still staring.

Katherine returned from the dining room and took the plates. "She's still shy around him?"

"I suppose that'll eventually stop." Danielle pulled out knives and forks and then closed the drawer with her hip. "Pastor Dan said to not force anything, especially with her so young, but—"

"It will be just fine. Look at Tyler." Katherine scooped the bags of food from the counter. "He's practically floating he's so happy."

"He is." Danielle smiled across the width of the house, where Jonas had gone back to watching her again. "*This* is Katherine."

"Katherine," Jonas repeated. "The older sister."

"Yes, that would be me." Katherine began passing the plates around the table. "I'm not staying for very long," she told him. "Tomorrow you'll meet all of us. Are you ready for that?"

"Ready." Jonas nodded once with his lopsided smile.

"We're a scary bunch, but not dangerous." Katherine smiled at him. "Jack, my husband, is looking forward to seeing you again."

"Jack. Jack from up the street in Glendale." Jonas smiled. "I was the new kid in third grade and he let me play basketball with him. I can remember going to high school and driver's education and all kinds of things like that. But not this." He looked around him.

Danielle saw the pain in his eyes when he turned toward her. "It'll come, Jonas. One step at a time. I have faith you will remember everything. You just can't push it. You'd better come to the table, both of you. Do you need help?"

"I can do it." He put down the photo album and began to struggle with his walker.

Tyler, such a good little boy, grabbed the walker by the handle. "Let me help, Dad. I'm real strong."

"Real strong," Jonas agreed, kind even when pain lined his pale face. "Thanks, buddy."

Danielle's vision blurred and she finished setting the table. The man toiling with his walker, scooting forward one slow step at a time, reached the table exhausted.

"I'll let myself out," Katherine said quietly from the kitchen. "Jonas, I'm going to keep praying for you."

"Th-thank you." He looked weary as he eased into the chair.

When she laid her hand on his big shoulder, Danielle

could feel the tension corded up like hard ropes. How difficult this had to be for him, coming to a home and a life and a family he could not remember. He was weak and wounded and not the man he was. He must have been able to see that, she realized now, seeing himself in the photo album.

A downside she hadn't anticipated.

Aching for him, she left her hand on his shoulder and kept the contact between them. "Goodbye, Kath, and thanks again."

Katherine glanced over her shoulder as she snagged her designer purse from the counter. "I'll see you all tomorrow. Good night, and, Jonas, it's so good to see you home."

Danielle felt her husband nod in acknowledgment, but her heart was too full of emotions too complicated to sort out. Tyler was climbing into his chair at the table, and Madison was mutinously—although adorably—running after her departing aunt, then looking at her parents, who were not acknowledging her mutiny, and her lower lip stuck out farther.

"All right! Mexi-fries!" Tyler pumped his fist in victory. "I getta say grace. Can I? *Please?*"

"If it's all right with your dad." It felt fantastic to say that again, but Jonas only looked at her bewildered, as if he had no idea why it would or wouldn't be his call. So she answered in his place. "I guess it is. Let me get Madison to the table."

"No." Madison looked pretty determined as she studied her father. She clutched her cell phone tightly.

"C'mon, *ple-eeeeese.*" Tyler was about to burst with so much excitement. "Daddy, she's been like this a lot. I'm tryin' to be a good big brother, but it's hard."

"I can see that," Jonas said quietly with a wink.

Not willing to scoop the child up and risk a meltdown, Danielle knelt to size up the situation. "Don't you want Mexi-fries?"

Madison bobbed her head once in a serious nod. Her tiara winked as it caught the overhead light.

"Then come to the table, princess." Danielle held out her hand, palm up, hoping for a little toddler cooperation.

Madison turned her serious gaze to her daddy on the far side of the table. "I wanna sit by yew, Mommy."

Over the top of their daughter's head, she could see the hurt on Jonas's face. As little as Madison was, she knew there was something different—much different—about the father who'd come home to them. Tyler was too excited to truly notice, but would his security be blown apart when he did?

I'll cross that bridge when I get there, she reminded herself. Prayer, tonight, would help as it always did. With the Lord's grace, perhaps Jonas would recover quickly enough that Tyler wouldn't realize it. Jonas had already defied the doctor's dim prognosis so far. Yes, she decided, steeling her spine, she would rely on her faith. God would make this right.

"I'll scoot your chair closer to mine, how's that?" Danielle waited for Madison to consider this. When the toddler placed her sticky little hand on hers, Danielle sighed with relief. One tantrum avoided. "Good girl. Let's get you up. Look at Tyler. You're making him wait."

"Hurry, Maddy," Tyler added, helping out. "We're all gettin' shorter. We need Mexi-fries now!"

A family joke, but Jonas's forehead furrowed as if he were trying to make sense of that. She'd tell him later about the joke of how the deep-fried Tater Tots kept a person from shrinking, she thought, as she buckled Madison in.

The instant she dropped into her own seat, she could feel the exhaustion in her muscles and bones. She folded her hands and bowed her head just in time, for Tyler was already saying—or more accurately, shouting—grace.

"Thanks for the eats, Lord! God bless us every one!" Tyler, proud of himself, added, "Amen!"

"Volume, kiddo," she reminded him after she'd added her own *amen.* "You don't need to shout. God can hear you just fine."

"Yeah, but He's all the way up in the sky. When Uncle Spence was on the roof cleaning the gutters, remember how loud I had to talk so's he could hear me?" Tyler helped himself to the tub of Mexi-fries. He dumped a generous portion on his plate. "The sky is really far up."

How could she argue with that? She took the tub from him and added Mexi-fries to her and Madison's plates, before she realized Jonas's plate remained empty.

"I'll help you, too," she said quietly. "Let me get the kids dished up."

He looked away, his eyes veiled, his face like stone. Tyler was chatting away, trying to decide from the options of tacos and nachos and burritos. Madison talked over the top of him, wanting her "taccas."

As she unwrapped Madison's chicken soft taco and cut it into quarters, and then helped Tyler search through the bags for the tacos that were his, she tried to keep the sadness from her heart. She'd known it would be like this. The doctors had been clear and had been warning her through the long journey of Jonas's recovery.

Everything had changed. There were no more loving looks across the table between them, and no more knowing looks that meant they were storing up cute things the kids were doing to be talked about and laughed over afterward. There were no mutual conversations about his day at work or hers at home with the kids, the way there always used to be. There was just silence and the typical noises that came from having two small children at the table.

She hadn't realized the depth of their love, and the importance of the meaningful bond that linked her spirit to his, until it was gone. Until there was nothing but silence between two strangers, with their children between them. That meant the love they'd shared was gone, too.

She quietly circled the table and unwrapped the two chicken burritos for Jonas and added a heap of Mexi-fries to his plate. Her footsteps echoed in the silence as she retraced the path back to her chair.

"No! No! No! No—ooooooo!" Madison's declaration of independence rang in the main bathroom at high enough decibel levels to break city ordinances. "I kin do it!"

Danielle slumped onto the closed lid of the toilet, dripping wet from helping her daughter with her bath. The steam had frizzed her hair, and she felt wilted as she rested her face in her hands. Steam swirled around her, driven by the current from the door swinging open and a half-clad Madison pounding across the hall to her bedroom. There was a yanking sound as she dragged open the lower drawer in her little white dresser.

"Mom? Are you okay?" Tyler asked from the doorway. She pasted a smile on her weary face and rose to her feet. "Absolutely. It's your turn, tiger. Would you fetch a clean towel and washcloth from the laundry room for me?"

"Okay!" He ran out of the room and down the hall.

"Don't run in the house," she reminded him and listened for his stampede to slow a bit.

She forced her feet forward, wondering how the rest of the evening would turn out for her and Jonas. They would be alone for the first time, and she was feeling nervous about being with him. It made no sense, and she didn't like the way she was feeling. But there it was, the hard ball of anxiety stuck in her midsection.

The evening had passed pleasantly with Tyler's little-boy energy and Madison's cute chatter. Jonas had sat in the living room with the kids while she'd cleaned up the kitchen. The kids were so busy and active, they'd unwittingly filled up the first half of the evening. But now, the last half was looming ahead of her and she was at a loss as to how to face it.

She turned on the bathwater and adjusted the temperature before adding Tyler's blue-colored bubble bath to the rising water. Madison shrieked with glee across the hall, and while Danielle hesitated in the hallway wondering about Jonas, the sight of her half-dressed daughter digging out every last item from her bottom drawer took precedence. "You are troubles, bubbles."

Madison grinned, showing off her dimples. "I want my Ella pants."

"Sweetie, you definitely need pants." Danielle knelt and gave the pink Cinderella pajama shirt a tug at the hem to straighten it. "You got that on all by yourself?"

"Yip."

"You're a good dresser."

"Yip."

Danielle sorted through the items on the floor, folding them as she went. No sign of the matching pajama pants, so she tried the middle drawer. There they were, right on top, in all their pink glory among the folded-up socks. She chased Madison, caught her and helped her into the ruffly pink bottoms. There. One kid *almost* done for the day.

First, she had to turn off the bathwater, then she began turning back Madison's bedcovers, not sure if Madison was going to give an argument or not.

Tyler's footsteps preceded him down the hall. He poked his head into the room. "Daddy's sleepin'," he said, then thundered into the bathroom.

Sleeping? She knew Jonas hadn't made the trek down the hall to their bedroom yet. He would have had to pass by the bathroom and the kids' rooms. Did that mean he'd fallen asleep on the couch? "Okay, prayers, cutie."

Madison bent to her knees and steepled her little hands. Her tiara slipped forward—yes, it appeared she was still wearing it—and Danielle removed it as she knelt down beside her. She listened while Madison said her prayers and tucked her in with a kiss.

"My story, Mommy?" Madison used her puppy-dog look, rendering her completely impossible to say no to.

"Let me check on Tyler and your daddy first. You stay right there, okay, bubbles?"

"Yip."

A quick glance into the bathroom told her that Tyler was safe and sound, covered with bubbles and busy playing with his floating fire tanker that shot water all over the tile.

She reminded him to remember to wash before padding down the hallway, where she found Jonas stretched out and sound asleep on the couch.

The poor man. He had to be exhausted. Danielle hit the power off button on the TV remote and circled around to lift the warm fleece blanket off the back of the couch. He didn't stir. She'd wake him up later, after she got both kids put to bed. For now, she shook the blanket out and gently covered him.

Help him find his way back to me, please, Lord, she prayed in the darkness. She kissed her husband's forehead and tiptoed from the room.

Chapter Three

"Sorry."

Danielle glanced up from pouring Jonas a second cup of morning coffee. "What are you sorry for?"

"Falling asleep." He didn't look at her as he concentrated on wrapping his hands around his spoon. Long months of hard rehabilitation had helped, but his motor skills were still limited.

She popped open the top of the flavored coffee creamer and poured it for him and then added some into her own cup. "It was a big day for all of us yesterday, with you coming home."

"You're dis-disappointed." He stumbled on the word.

Since she couldn't admit that, not without hurting him, she set the carafe on the ruffled blue place mat at Tyler's empty place and slipped into the chair. "Are you?"

He gulped. "Could be easier."

She nodded, seeing now what she'd been too busy this morning to notice, getting Tyler ready for the church summer program and keeping Madison out of trouble.

Jonas had managed to dress himself in a sweatshirt and jeans, but the sweatshirt hung on him, twisted to the left. His feet beneath the table were in socks, not shoes. "I should have helped you more this morning. I'm sorry. I won't forget again."

"You helped enough." Jonas straightened his shoulders, as if his pride were involved, too. "The kids first."

"Yes. That's what we agreed back in Seattle, but—" She stared down into her steaming mug, unable to find any answers in the dark depths. She'd let him down, and that's the one thing she didn't want to do. Somehow she had to figure out a way to manage everything on her own. "It's going to be difficult for a while, but I don't mind working hard for you, Jonas. For the kids. For us."

He swallowed hard, as if her words mattered to him, and turned in his chair toward the wall. "Our wedding pictures."

"Yes." She looked at them, too. How young and carefree they seemed back then. On impulse, she rose and plucked the collage frame from the wall. "There are some of the reprints I framed up from that day. I should dig out our wedding album. It's in the closet somewhere out of reach, for safekeeping."

"You're smiling. It must have been a good day."

"One of the best of my life."

She laid the gold frame on the table, and he moved his coffee cup aside to make room. As they leaned forward to study the pictures together, she smelled the scent of his shampoo and the soap on his skin. Her heart cinched a notch. Yes, she thought, tenderly, he was still her Jonas. "If you notice, you're smiling, too."

"Yep. I look pretty happy."

"You were."

She touched her fingertip to the glass frame, where they'd just parted from sharing their first kiss as man and wife. Hand in hand, they stood smiling, facing their family and friends with the jeweled light from the sun-drenched stained glass gracing them. Their happiness was palpable, so shining and new. "I wish you could remember how that felt to finally be married. To be together with the whole world at our feet."

"Was our marriage good?"

She noticed the concern in his eyes, the sadness on his face and the wonder. It was not fair that one bullet had stolen so much from him. At least she had the memories of their love. At least she knew what they could have again. "It was very good."

"We were close."

"Yes. Very close."

He nodded once in acknowledgment but not in understanding.

How did she tell him that was her greatest fear? That they might never find one another again. They might never again share that rare close bond they'd had. Grief stabbed deep into her soul, and she fought it away. She had to keep her faith strong and believe that God would not forsake them. "We were best friends. Best…everything."

"E-very-thing." Jonas lingered over that word, as if he were trying to figure out what that meant. He remained bent over the pictures.

She moved away and took the carafe with her to rinse in the sink. All around them, hung on the walls or in stand-alone frames or snapshots tacked to their refrigerator, were photographs of their life together, of the babies and of the kids growing up. Of a happier time—her soul ached with sadness for the loss of that happy, innocent time when Jonas was whole.

It wasn't fair to keep wishing for the past, she thought as she turned to the sink, rinsed out the pot and slipped it into the top rack of the dishwasher. Out of the corner of her eye, she saw Jonas struggling to stand, his attention focused on one of the photographs on the wall. She leaned a little to see what he stared at with such fascination. Her heart stopped when she recognized the picture. It was of her, propped up in a hospital bed, exhausted from forty-one hours of labor and cradling their precious son in her arms.

He did not remember that day, she realized, or how happy they were and how proud he was. She closed the dishwasher quietly, feeling reality settle into the damaged places in her heart.

When he looked away, she saw his eyes were silvered with tears. Tears that did not fall as he blinked them away and straightened his shoulders. Strong—that was her Jonas, always strong.

"I'll help you to remember," she promised him with all the strength and faith in her soul. "It's going to be all right."

In the corner, untouched by the sunlight that tumbled through the big picture window, Jonas nodded. He didn't look as if he believed her. Not one bit.

There was a knock at the front door—the quick tap-tap of her mom's signature knock. Already her key was in the lock and the doorknob was turning. The security system chimed as the front door swung open. Danielle straightened, turned off the faucet and reached for the dish towel to dry her hands.

"Knock, knock. Hello!" Dorrie's smile was bright, as always. She was a wonder and an incredible mother.

Danielle knew she paled by comparison. "Come on in. I just washed out the coffeepot. I can make fresh."

"I had my morning quota, my dear. Jonas, it's great to see you home—" Her pleasant voice was drowned out by Madison shouting from the living room.

"Grammy! Grammy! Grammy!" Bare feet padded on the carpet and then on the linoleum as the little girl—today a mermaid—burst into sight, flinging her arms wide and wrapping them tightly around her grandmother's knees.

"Hi, honey. Are you going to let Grammy take you to your swimming lessons?"

"Yip. I kin blow bubbles and kick!" Soft brown curls tumbled over her shoulders as she leaned her head back to grin up at her grandmother.

"I can't wait to see. Do you have your bag all packed?"

Danielle chimed in. "I got it half-finished. It's on the foot of her bed, I just have to grab a towel."

"I'll do that. No worries. What time is Jonas's appointment?"

"Nine-thirty." Danielle glanced at the clock on the stove. "We should leave in a few minutes."

"I'll finish up here, too. That's why I'm here, to help out. I'll have lunch all ready when you get back. Jonas, I hope you still like tuna casserole."

"Y-yes." Jonas was struggling with his walker to get around the table. His left leg was very stiff.

She resisted the need to run to his side. For him it was a matter of pride.

He ambled toward her, but his gaze was on their little

daughter, in her mermaid shirt and matching pants, her soft curls and sweetness.

"Madison," he said. "I like to swim, too."

The little girl's eyes widened, and she sidled around to hide behind her grandmother. She stared at Jonas and didn't say anything at all.

Danielle couldn't breathe for the pain in her heart. Madison had Jonas wrapped around her little finger since the moment she'd come into the world.

Jonas shuffled forward, but it was the sadness in his eyes that both kept her silent and that gave her hope as he eased alongside his walker. He had one hand on the edge of the counter and the other on the walker's grip.

"You don't like this?" he asked the toddler, nodding at the metal appliance.

From behind her grandmother's knee, Madison shook her head again, scattering her soft curls. "No!"

"Me, either." He took a shaky step away, unsteady as he shuffled forward without much support.

She was across the kitchen, holding her husband's elbow without thought, but he didn't lean on her. No, no matter how much support Jonas needed, he would not do that. He did allow her to keep him steady at this crucial moment as he went a few uncertain inches forward.

Their little girl took a cautious step out from behind her grandmother, looking relieved the scary metal thing had been left behind.

Jonas leaned forward and held out his hand, a father's devotion sincere and quiet. He waited while Madison bit her bottom lip, debating the merits of approaching her daddy now.

When Madison looked up to her, Danielle nodded and smiled. "It's okay, honey," she said and scrunched down a bit to be more at the toddler's level.

Encouraged, Madison took a step toward her daddy. "Why you got that?"

Jonas's smile was wobbly and looked relieved. "Because my leg doesn't work so well. But it's gonna be better."

"Oh. Okeydokey." Madison laid her hand on his, studying him trustingly. "You gonna come see me swim? I kin kick real fast! Jest like a mermaid."

"I'd sure like to see that sometime soon."

"Yip." Madison grinned hugely. "C'mon, Grammy! I shew you my towel!"

Danielle rose to full height as the little girl grabbed her grandmother by the hand and pulled her through the kitchen. She was thankful, deeply grateful.

She turned to Jonas, who waited until Madison was out of sight before he grabbed for the edge of the counter. She tugged his walker to him, holding him steady. He looked too tired from the effort and his leg was shaking, but his smile was pure Jonas.

"This is going to work out just fine," she told him, certain of it now. "You wait and see."

"I brought my toolbox," Dad said in his gruff, good-guy way as he shouldered through the front door and stomped his boots on the entry rug. "Figure the boys and I can get a few things done for you around here."

Danielle looked up from the counter where she was peeling carrots for the salad. Her burdens lifted at simply seeing her father—her stepfather, who'd adopted her when he'd married her mother long ago. Gratitude filled her right up. She couldn't have a better father, and she loved him. "Dad, this is supposed to be a celebration dinner. You shouldn't be doing work around here. We can worry about things getting done later."

"Nonsense. You know me. I'm not happy unless I'm busy." He winked, and his smile was good-natured as always. "Might as well make myself useful while I'm here. And what about you, missy?"

"What about me?"

He set down his toolbox against the entryway wall. "You sure you ought to be in here working like that? Your mother isn't gonna be happy if she and the kids come back from the grocery store and see that you aren't taking it easy like she told you to."

"I'm fine, Dad. Really." She smiled to prove it to him. "You know me. I'm not happy unless I'm busy."

He shook his head slowly from side to side and, judging by the squint to his friendly blue eyes, he wasn't fooled one bit. "Jonas resting?"

"He fell asleep on the couch. He had a tough physical therapy session." Not to mention the doctor appointment before that. "Let me get you something cool to drink, Dad. It's a scorcher out there."

"Looked like it was trying to storm to me."

"Storm?" That couldn't be good news. She hadn't had time to check any weather report. Apparently she'd been too busy trying to get a start on dinner prep to look out the big garden window over the sink and counter.

Now that she did look, she saw thunderheads were gathering on the horizon. Huge ones. That might not bode well for their backyard picnic. And for her not to have noticed, well, it only went to show how tired she felt.

Great. She squared her drooping shoulders and put down the peeler. "I'll get you some iced tea."

"I'll do it myself, missy." Dad ambled her way, still a big man despite the fact that he'd passed retirement age. "But I will take one of those brownies. They smell awful good."

Danielle reached for a clean knife and joined him at the opposite counter to cut him a generous piece. "You're going to spoil your appetite."

"Yeah, I know." Dad was smiling as he tore a paper towel from the dispenser and held it to use in place of a plate. "No one anywhere makes a better brownie than you. You even got Ava beat."

One of her younger sisters, Ava, was a professional baker. A high compliment, but one she'd heard before. Plus, Dad was generous with compliments. She kissed his cheek. "Why don't you go put up your feet? If you don't want to disturb Jonas, you can use the TV either in the basement or in our room."

"No, I don't mind bothering Jonas." Dad winked as he strode out of sight. The faint rumble of his voice in the living room told her that Jonas must have woken up.

When she peered around the corner to check on him, he had straightened up on the couch. Now sitting up, he was sleepy-looking and pale, but he seemed glad of the company. That had to be a good sign, right? She worried about the evening ahead. Her family—bless them—had dearly wanted to see Jonas again. But was he up to so much at once?

Well, they would find out. She hoped so. She wanted

him to see that he wasn't as alone as he had to feel. She leaned her shoulder against the archway to watch as Jonas talked with her father, someone else he didn't remember. But within moments they were both smiling and talking like old friends.

Great. She blew out a breath of relief and went back to her carrots. The men's voices rumbled pleasantly as she finished peeling and dug the pitcher of iced tea out of the refrigerator.

The house was relatively quiet without the little ones— Mom had taken them with her on her grocery run. She missed Tyler's constant motion and Madison's constant chatter underfoot. And thinking of the kids made her remember how it used to be—how Jonas would always hang around the kitchen and help her, grazing on whatever was handy to snack on.

Hard to imagine, since Jonas and her dad had once been close.

There was a knock at the front door, a few quick, no-nonsense raps and then a key turned in the lock. Spence, the oldest of the clan, poked his head in. "Hit the garage door opener for me, would ya? I'll get the front yard mowed before Dad thinks of it."

"Thank you, Spence."

"Don't mention it." He shut the door firmly.

The oven timer chose that moment to beep. She hit the off button, snagged an oven mitt from the closest drawer. She knelt to lift the casserole pot of baked beans from the oven and onto a trivet on the counter. While she heard Dad and Jonas talking, she tried not to focus on her husband's halting words—that halting was worse when he was tired, she'd learned. She ached for him.

This was not fair. She had to lay aside her anger at the desperate gunman who had fired that shot. Jonas hadn't deserved that, and yet it had happened just the same. She rushed around to the inside garage door and caught sight of him on the couch—struggling to find the right words while Dad waited patiently.

No, she thought, her heart heavy. This was not fair. Surely there was some good that would come out of this—some good the Lord would find in all this hardship. But for the life of her Danielle couldn't figure out what. She yanked open the inside door and hit the button.

The churn of the opener's engine drowned out the sound of her husband's voice. As the door lifted, there was Spence, in T-shirt and denims, storming into the garage like a hulk. His grimace was hardly a grimace at all, which meant he must be in a very good mood. He grabbed the lawn mower and wheeled it out into the driveway. The roar of the engine coming to life echoed in the garage.

Talk about a reliable guy. Danielle loved her brother. She couldn't have a better one—or a better family, and she thanked the Lord for them every day. She'd just hoped there would be less need for their help after Jonas's homecoming. They'd done so much. They had to be exhausted, too.

She heard the air conditioner click on and felt the swirl of cooled air against her ankles and shut the door, leaving it unlocked so Spence could find his way in after his mowing. She remembered the kitchen work awaiting her. She wanted to get it done so that her mom didn't have any choice; she couldn't help with dinner because it would already be done. Mom had done more than her share already.

It was Jonas's voice, low and sonorous, that made her

stop halfway to the kitchen. Seeing him so changed still hit her hard every time.

"Is that right, John? Yellowstone, you say?"

"Yep," Dad was saying. Always brief on words but long on heart. "You said the RV drove real fine. Yep, real fine."

"I'm sure it did. Don't remember it."

"Well, it did."

Jonas noticed her standing there and it was hard to tell by the look on his face if he was glad to see her or not. When he looked at her, he had to feel more pressure to remember. And that was the last thing she wanted. He had pressure enough.

"Dani." Dad turned in the chair and winked at her. "I'm gonna take Jonas with me."

"What? Where?" Jonas looked confused. Maybe a little panicked.

He might not remember that she was always on his side. That she would never forsake him, even when it came to her own family. "Dad, Jonas might not be up to working with tools yet."

"Tools?" Jonas's eyes widened in surprise.

He could not know that it was a family thing, he and Dad and Spence, always eager to fix what was broken. He would not remember how it used to be, that when Dad assumed Jonas's help in all kinds of family construction projects, Jonas would find a moment to come up to her and lean close so that only she could hear. He would say in that affable way of his, "I don't remember getting my draft notice."

No, Jonas did not have any idea how they would chuckle quietly together before he would go off to help her dad.

Now, Jonas seemed uncertain, but when he looked down

at his hands she realized why. After so much nerve damage, he could not handle carpenter tools. What could she do to reassure him? "Dad, you give Jonas a rest on this one. He's recuperating. He can watch if he wants to and keep you company, but it might be better if he rests."

"Yep. Gotcha." Dad nodded once and rose to his feet as if that were settled. "Well, what do you say, Jonas? You want to come keep an eye on me?"

"You need it." Humor glinted in his hazel eyes, and his lopsided grin could not be dearer.

Danielle felt hope buoy her. "I'll bring back some tea for both of you."

"Thanks, missy." Dad scooted Jonas's walker closer within reach. "C'mon, son, we've got work to do."

"Yes, sir." Jonas struggled to his feet and winked at her over the top of her dad's head.

Danielle practically floated to the kitchen, full of gratitude that her whole family was together again.

Chapter Four

Over the noise at the dinner table, Danielle heard her grandmother lean over to Jonas and say, "How is it that you are still so handsome?"

A blush pinkened his cheeks, making him even more good-looking. "Just luck."

That made Gran chuckle in that light, joyful way of hers.

Danielle looked up from cutting Madison's hot dog, and her pulse turned heavy, as if she had peanut butter in her veins. Could he be remembering? Just luck. That was what Jonas always used to say whenever Gran would ask that question. Wouldn't that be perfect if he did remember? If he did defy the doctors' dim prognoses for his memory loss, too?

"Mommy?" Madison tugged on her sleeve to get her attention. "I wanna biiig piece of cake. Pleeeease?"

"No, not yet and you know it, princess." Danielle scooped a generous spoonful of the potatoes au gratin that Katherine had brought. "I know you want these."

"Taters!" The little girl agreed cheerfully and flashed

her dimples, confident that she was adorable and had more than one person's attention at the table.

Katherine peered around Madison's head on her other side. "Let me take over for you. I would love to *and* I'm closer to the taters."

"Thanks." Danielle handed over the cartoon character, child-sized fork.

It was wonderful to see her sister so happy. Marriage suited her, and Jack was the right kind of husband—good, strong and loving, a man who always did the right thing. It was another of her prayers answered. And as she scanned the table, she saw nothing but a testimony to that wondrous power. Katherine wasn't the only newlywed sister at the table.

There were her younger twin sisters. Ava had Brice at her side, chattering away to him and to Tyler. Amusement and love mixed together as Brice watched her with a besotted grin on his face. They'd married in the spring, and Ava was always the happy sort, but she practically shone like the sun these days. Love and married life had transformed her.

Aubrey, although identical to Ava, couldn't have been more different. She was quieter, and so was her husband-to-be, William. Their love was a tacit statement that still waters ran deep. Their wedding was coming up soon, and they had included the kids in their wedding party.

Lauren, home now from California, was finishing her master's in business at the local campus. She and Caleb had married last month in a sweet May ceremony that had been as low-key and as lovely as Lauren herself.

"Mommy! Guess what?" Tyler called out across the table.

She blinked, drawn out of her thoughts. She focused on her little boy's face and recognized that wide-eyed excited expression. Ava and Brice had been talking about their dog to him. "What?"

"If I had a dog, do you know what? Then Rex wouldn't be lonesome when he came over here."

Rex, the mentioned golden retriever, popped his head up from beneath the table to shine his puppy dog eyes on her.

Help, she wanted to plead silently to Jonas, but that bond between them was no longer there. She couldn't look at her husband and have him know instinctively what she needed. He would not be coming to her rescue. She sighed, lonely. How could she be otherwise? She missed her husband. "We'll talk about a dog later, cutie."

"Yeah, but…I gotta lot of reasons why we should get a dog." Tyler looked so hopeful.

"I know. You keep making that list, okay?"

"Yeah." He breathed out a long sigh. It was hard being a kid and dogless.

Across the table, Spence nodded to her, as if in agreement. He was not fond of dogs, especially near the table. Poor Spence. He had a good heart but had a hard time letting it show. It was no surprise to his family or anyone who knew him that he hadn't found a woman who could look past the gruffness to the sweet man inside. And, if he kept going, she was afraid he never would.

But it was the empty chair next to Spence that troubled her. Rebecca—the youngest—was late. Again. And, as experience had taught them all, that could only mean one thing—trouble with that boyfriend of hers, Chris. What if this serious relationship took a more serious turn? It was something that turned Danielle's stomach cold. Chris was the kind of young man who seemed nice—there was never anything specifically he'd done that made her dislike him. Except for the fact he was not entirely nice to Rebecca.

Rebecca, who saw only the good in everyone, couldn't see it.

Gran's merry voice broke into her thoughts. "Jonas, they tell me you aren't remembering things so well. You're not alone, boy. It happens to the best of us. Do you remember me?"

"Nope. Not a thing."

"Then you don't know how you and Dani met."

"N-no. I do not."

Danielle plainly read the shame on her husband's face. She placed her hand on his shoulder, still so wide and strong. "Gran likes to think she's the reason we're together."

Jonas quirked his brow. "That so, Gran?"

The elderly woman, so rosy and dear, chuckled warmly. "Your marriage is a testimony to the power of prayer. My husband was still with me back then, and one night, when we were just back from snowbirding in Scottsdale, we met with Ann and Silas Donovan, Brice's grandparents. We were all in the same boat. We had grandchildren but no great-grandchildren. I saw this as a totally unacceptable situation, so I decided to take it to the good Lord and start praying."

"Is that so?" Jonas didn't seem to understand that it was their marriage, and their firstborn son, who'd been that long-awaited great-grandchild.

"You'd just moved into the rental house on Caleb's grandparents' property just down the road," Danielle explained, remembering that sweet summer they'd met.

"That so?" He grinned. "I lived down the road from Gran?"

"You did." He'd always called "Gran" by her first name,

Mary, but she didn't correct him. She reached for his knife and began to cut into his barbecued chicken. "It was this nice little two-bedroom house with a perfect view of Gran's horse pastures, where I rode with Aubrey every morning."

"I see." He still couldn't tell the twins apart, and looked at Ava, who was giggling away at something Tyler was saying. "It's my guess I took one look at you and decided to take you to dinner."

"And you were awfully confident about it, too." Danielle felt the cold places within her warm like that June morning. She wished he could remember how that day had changed both of their lives for the better.

"Confident? What did I do?" He watched her blankly, his gaze searching her face. A stranger's gaze.

But he was no stranger to her. Gone was the memory they shared of how she'd first set eyes on the young, strapping twenty-two-year-old Jonas, so handsome and friendly and good. She'd been afraid to trust him. Repeating the heartbreak of her mother's first marriage had been her fear back then—her natural father had been violent to her.

Did she tell him how nervous he'd made her? Or how secretly wonderful she thought he was, even at first glance? "I'll never forget how you strolled up to the fence one morning after Aubrey and I were back from a long ride, and you had your arms braced on the top rail and a cowboy hat shading your face. Just the impression you gave made me turn my horse around and avoid you entirely."

"No, you didn't. That's a good one. A good joke."

"It's no joke, handsome. I thought you were trouble spelled with a capital *T.*" She had to laugh at herself, fighting against the pull of sadness. How could he not remember?

How could so much love and life be wiped clean like images off a blackboard? "Okay, so I was wrong."

"Am I trouble?" Jonas asked, as if he had no clue what that meant.

"Big-time," she assured him. She wished he could see how blue the sky was and how vibrant and stalwart he had looked with the mountains behind him.

"How long did you stay away from me?"

Now he had the wrong impression. She should have said that she'd wanted to avoid him because she was scared. Sometimes when you looked your dream in the face, nothing was more terrifying.

Before she could answer, Gran did. "Didn't I mention that I had to resort to prayer?"

"She didn't like me *that* much?"

"In my defense—" Danielle set down his knife and then reached for her own "—I was looking for a nice guy to marry. Someone as wonderful as Dad."

"We're a rare bunch," Dad called out from across the table.

Jonas looked puzzled. "I'm a nice guy. Right?"

"The nicest," she reassured him. "But I didn't know you. And a handsome, self-assured man who had too much charm for his own good didn't fit with what I was searching for."

"I've got charm, huh?" He gave her that lopsided grin.

"A tad." Danielle smiled, unable to find the words to describe how deeply he had charmed her.

"A smidgen," Ava called from across the table.

"Just a pinch," Aubrey chimed in. "I told Dani at the time that she ought to go for it, to go talk to you, but she whispered back to me that you probably weren't a Christian, so forget it."

"Did I look like I wasn't a Christian?" Jonas sounded even more puzzled, although his eyes twinkled.

So, he was teasing her. She deserved it. "I was afraid that you weren't, and that meant I wasn't going to let you charm me into accepting a dinner date."

"Good thing I did."

"Yes, you did charm me. Eventually, but I made you work for it."

Gran finished the story for him. "Son, you had to come by the pasture every morning for a week until you got smart and met her at the gate on my property that led to the stable. She had to talk to you because you were in her way. I remember you held the gate open for the girls and their horses. When you showed up at church the next morning, then she stopped avoiding you as much."

"As much? She didn't like me."

"I just thought you were too good to be true, Jonas." She laid her hand on his. Gone was the connection she'd once felt to him—that emotional bond between their hearts. They were strangers again. "As soon as I figured out, I let you talk me into going out with you."

"Lucky me."

Jonas. She didn't know how to tell him how wrong he was. That she had been the lucky one—and still was.

"All that time," Gran went on to say, "I was praying you two kids would take a liking to one another. I figured prayer was my only hope with the rate you two were going."

"But I won her." Jonas looked at her with a touch of pride and a dash of wonder.

"Yes, handsome, you won me." She ached remembering the excitement of that time, of getting ready for her first date with him, of being carried away with—and afraid of—the possibilities. She'd been both thrilled and terrified that he was *The One*.

"No-ooo. I kin do it!" Madison's declaration rose above everyone's table conversations.

"She reminds me of someone," Mom commented across the table. "Hmm, let me think of who that could be—"

Everyone laughed—everyone but Jonas. He was still looking at her, watching her as if seeing her for the first time.

She slipped her hand in his under the table. He held on to her so tight.

"Cake! Coming through!" With two dessert plates in hand, Ava sauntered through the maze of the living room.

Danielle recognized the deep chocolate cake—Ava's to-die-for triple-chocolate dream cake. She knew it was pointless to resist. Her waistline was going to take a hit. "Thanks, Ava. I love the pink frosting."

"I made it in honor of the princess. Sorry, Jonas." Ava set the plates on the coffee table. Her blond hair was still tied back in a ponytail and she wore her work clothes— jeans and a bright yellow T-shirt that advertised, Every Kind of Heaven Bakery. "But I did save the best pieces for you, Jonas. It has lots of frosting. Rebecca still hasn't made it yet, so you don't have to fight her for it."

Danielle scooted closer, keeping her voice low. "Is that the call Mom took?"

"Yep. Rebecca said she might not make it, but not to worry. Everything is okeydokey, but I don't believe her. Do you?"

Danielle worried; she couldn't help it. She would say extra prayers for Rebecca tonight.

"Do you know what you two need?" Ava squinted at her and then at Jonas.

Uh-oh. Danielle recognized that look. "I'm not sure I want to know."

"You two need a date night. I mean big-time huge. How long has it been?"

"Since before Jonas was injured." It was hard to think back that far, past the fog of the last difficult year, to when life had been normal. Crazy and busy and hectic, but normal.

"Face it, you both deserve a break. One of us will babysit, right, Aubrey?"

"Sure, because I have all this free time with the wedding coming up," Aubrey gently joked from across the room. "But, Dani, if I can squeeze out some time, it's yours."

Her sisters, always there for her. She loved them for it.

"I know," Ava argued back cheerfully. "We'll get Rebecca to do it. She's not here to argue."

"Exactly," Aubrey agreed with a wink. "I'll have to give her a call later and tell her we volunteered her."

Those two. Danielle caught the amused expression on her husband's face. She might not know what he was thinking, but he was clearly getting a kick out of the twins. Most people did. She also saw something else on his face. Did that gleam in his eyes mean he was happy?

He leaned closer to her and his arm bumped her shoulder. "Go on a date? But we're married."

"Yes, but we used to go out, just you and me, without the kids. For some alone time." A date night. Maybe it would help his memory. Hope rose up within her. "We could go to your favorite restaurant."

"My favorite restaurant." Trouble—humor—flashed in

Jonas's dark eyes. "Now, pretty lady, I don't know what my favorite restaurant is. You could tell me anyplace."

"And you'd never know?" Danielle nodded, feeling lighter and lighter. She winked. "It didn't occur to me, but thanks for mentioning that. I think I can use this to my advantage."

"Yep. I need to keep a—what is it?—my eyes on you." He winked. "A real hardship."

Had he just paid her a compliment? Was he flirting with her? Her heart sweetly fluttered. She felt for a moment the way she had for their first date—all sugary anticipation and pie-in-the-sky hope.

Over at the table with Aubrey, Madison's shout of glee rose across the living room and above the rest of the conversations in the living room, and Tyler's laughter joined his sister's. It had been a long time since such happy sounds rang loud in this house, without a note of sadness to weigh them down.

That had to be another sign from the Lord, Danielle decided, determined and resolute. She believed hard enough to make everything all right. It was going to be. Really. She was going to have her husband back again. And the children their father.

If a tiny niggling of doubt existed beneath her resolve, she did her best to rub it out and cling to her faith. It *had* to be okay. She didn't know if her heart could take more hardship.

"That settles it, Dani." Dorrie set two plates of cake on the TV trays in front of Gran and Dad. "I'm babysitting next Friday night so you two kids can have a night out together, just like you always used to do."

"We did?" Jonas turned to her for confirmation.

"Nearly every week, thanks to our very generous family. There's always someone to watch the kids for us."

Jonas seemed satisfied at that and turned to his plate and fumbled awkwardly with the fork.

She wasn't going to focus on all that he couldn't remember. That those loving, fun, close evenings they'd spent together, just the two of them, were gone to him. They were not gone to her. No, her love and her memories of their marriage were strong enough for the two of them.

Later, after everyone was gone, leaving the house in some semblance of order, the kids were bathed and asleep—finally—in their beds, she was alone with Jonas. He was still awake on the couch, the TV's glow making a soft light, but it wasn't the TV he was watching. He had the photo album open on his knees.

"We went to Yellowstone," he said when she entered the room. "My parents took me there when I was ten. We went on vacation every summer until their car accident." He paused, as if searching for the word. "This vacation was my favorite. Good memories."

"We have good memories of there, too, as a family. I wish you could remember."

"Maybe one day."

"Maybe." Danielle studied the picture they'd taken of the four of them crowded around the Yellowstone sign at the entrance to the park. They had laughed a lot that day.

"Did you really not like me?"

His question surprised her. She eased onto the edge of the coffee table to face him. "I don't think I've ever not liked you."

"Gran said—" He paused, his forehead crinkling in thought. "You didn't like me."

"Do you mean when I would avoid you in the horse

pasture?" She waited for him to nod, realizing how that must seem to him. "It wasn't that I didn't like you. I took one look at you and liked you."

"You did?" He lit up at that, grinning lopsidedly at her.

Okay, that felt like old times, too, the blessed way things used to be. "I wasn't joking when I said you looked too good to be true."

In a blink, the memory came back to her with all its feelings, colors and life. How sweet the field smelled with the gentle morning breezes stirring it. The whoosh of the wind in her ears and the feel of the horse beneath her. The cheerful joy of the meadowlarks and pheasants faded to silence.

She would never forget how the crisp brightness of the newly rising sun faded when she first glimpsed the tall, wide-shouldered man at the fence line. Even with his face shaded by a Stetson, her heart had taken a plunge from her chest all the way down to her toes. It was as if she'd known, soul-deep, that this man would change her life.

"I was being cautious," she told him, remembering the feeling of falling, as if Muffin, her horse, had sent her tumbling. "What I felt for you was so strong, although I didn't even know you. I was afraid of making a mistake and of getting hurt."

"Love at first sight?"

She looked into the innocent question of his eyes and realized how hard this had to be for him. To be bereft of all the memories that had made up his life, which had gotten him here, which made him—and them—who they were. She laid her hand on his, and the deep connection they'd built together by loving one another every day of their marriage was not there. Not even with her memories and all the love she held in her heart for him. Sadness filled her.

"Yes," she answered patiently. "It was love at first sight. That's a frightening thing, because love can make you blind. You don't remember all that I've told you over the years about my real father."

"No," Jonas answered sadly, gently.

Making it easy to face the dreaded past again. "He was not good to my mom or to me. Rebecca was just a toddler when he left, so she doesn't remember how bad it was. How miserable we all were. And my mom, she did everything she could to protect us from his anger. He was a very angry and self-centered man, and she took the brunt of it. His leaving was one of the best blessings of my young life, at the time. Gaining John as a stepdad was even better. I—"

She closed her eyes against the bleak memories, willing them to vanish forever. "I didn't want to make my mother's mistakes. There's good in everyone, even those who behave badly, just as my biological father did, and I was afraid I would only see the good. Until it was too late."

Jonas nodded, seeming thoughtful. "When did you— decide I wasn't so b-bad?"

"When I saw you in church that next Sunday, I ran out of excuses." She could remember the cool feel of the smooth wooden pew as she wrapped her fingers around the edge of the seat, holding on so tightly when she saw handsome Jonas Lowell stride into the church. It had been a good thing that she was sitting down because her knees would have given out.

The sunshine had chosen that moment to brighten, spilling through the stained glass windows in rich, jeweled tones, spilling over him. Standing in those noble colors, Jonas was like the answer to her prayers. She had been asking the Lord for a good, wonderful man to love her for so long that she'd grown accustomed to waiting, to being safe without having to risk her heart. Without having to get so close to someone who could stop loving her the way her first dad had.

But she'd also had the influence of her stepdad—John McKaslin—in her life, so she knew, too, that there were men who stayed, who loved with all their hearts, who stood for what was right.

"Sitting there in the sanctuary surrounded by people I loved and trusted, it came to me that I was afraid. It went beyond being cautious, so I asked for the Lord's help. I gave up my fears to Him and vowed to try to follow where my answered prayers would lead me."

"I wasn't so bad." While his grin was back, his eyes remained sad for her. "Did I t-talk to you?"

"Yes. You came up after the service and when Dad invited you out to brunch with us, I took it as confirmation. You sat beside me in the restaurant and we just clicked. We talked as if we'd been friends all our lives, and there was something there, something rare that scared me. I think it was what I felt from the very start, when I first spotted you leaning up against the rail fence. It was like finding part of myself, the better half, and finding that I had come home. It's so frightening to accept, because it is so very much to lose. You are so very much to lose."

"You didn't lose me. I'm still here."

Her eyes welled with tears and a sob lodged in the middle of her throat. She felt the tangible weight of all the fear she had refused to let herself feel after Jonas was shot, all of the terror she locked away because it had been too overwhelming.

At the time, she'd pushed aside all her anguish because being calm and having a positive outlook for Jonas's sake was more important. But now it rolled over her like a tidal wave. No one really knew—not the doctors, not the well-meaning nurses, not even her family or their minister—how deeply she loved her husband.

Only God did, Who could see into her heart.

Jonas, however, could not—he no longer could—and only stared at her with a thousand questions in his eyes. "Tell me about our first date."

There was so much to say, so much more that couldn't be put into words. Love was like that, the greatest pieces of which could only be felt. "What do you want to know?"

"Did I ask you out after the brunch with your family?"

"No. You didn't get a chance to talk with me alone. My family kept butting in, nosy as always, bless them." She could feel the kiss of the summer sunshine on her face and smell the sweet scent of strawberries from that long-ago day drifting in from the farmer's fields across the road.

"They liked me at first?"

"They adored you. What I will always remember is the way you took my hand to help me into the car. Your hand was strong and tender all at once. You stood so tall next to me, and your hand was so big compared to mine. And your touch was intimate."

"How do you mean?"

"Like when our hands met, our spirits did, too."

He watched her with unblinking eyes, his gaze thoughtful, with realization on his face. "I was already in love with you, too. Love at first sight."

"That's what you told me, later." Happiness, that's what the pressure was, expanding painfully in her throat. The man before her, with a shaky smile and the side of his face still a touch paralyzed, with his slightly gnarled left hand and the walker tucked off to the side of the couch, was no longer a complete stranger. "Do you remember me at all, Jonas?"

"No. But I'm going to." He reached out and gathered her hands. His movements were slow, his touch tender, as he wrapped her hands with his.

She felt her heart tug. Her spirit awaken. Her soul sigh in recognition.

"I want to. Help me remember, Danielle."

She would not fail him. She hadn't given up on him in the hospital, when his survival had been nothing but the smallest chance. She would not let go of him now. "I will, Jonas. I promise you."

"Mommy!" Madison stood in the shadowed light of the hallway, scrubbing her sleepy eyes with her little fists. Her stuffed bunny was tucked in the crook of her arm. "I want some water. Minnie does, too."

"Okay, bubbles." It took a little piece out of her to withdraw her hand from Jonas's. Their moment was interrupted by the best possible reason, but the opportunity was not gone. They would have more time alone on their upcoming date night.

She scooped up their little girl, who had Jonas's eyes and her brown curls, and snuggled the warm, sleepy toddler close. She caught Jonas's gaze over the top of Madison's downy head. His look was amazingly full of warmth and tenderness and a deep, heartfelt wish.

A wish she could feel.

Thank the Lord they were on the same page, still wanting the same things in life. Jonas might be lost to her, but she believed not for much longer. Hope lifted her up as she took off for the kitchen.

Chapter Five

Jonas took the photo album marked Our Wedding off the closet shelf. Since he was ready for their date and waiting on Danielle, maybe this album would help. *Please, Lord, let me remember.*

He wished his foot didn't drag as he made his way across the bedroom floor. He wanted his hand to stop spasming as he eased down onto the overstuffed chair by the big window. If only he knew how to put the frustration he felt into words.

He wished for a lot of things these days, but he did not waste his prayers on himself. It was Danielle he thought of as he turned to the first page. It was Danielle he prayed for as he fought to find a single scrap of recognition in the professional-quality photograph of the two of them smiling together, hand in hand, wedding rings gleaming.

Please, Lord, let me remember for her sake.

It had been such a tough week. Their family minister, Pastor Green, had stopped him after the morning service and asked how he was adjusting to being back home.

"Fine, just ~~fine~~," he'd ~~told the minister~~, because ~~Danielle~~ had been at his side. He hadn't wanted her to hear the truth. She'd been beside him, holding on to his arm to steady him in the crowd. That killed him but he'd allowed it, not wanting to hurt her feelings. She kept watching him with those big brown eyes of hers, so sad and hopeful all at once. It destroyed him that he was letting her down.

Just fine *had* been the truth. At least, part of the truth; he hadn't lied to their pastor, but he hadn't added the whole truth, either. The unsaid words haunted him now. *Fine, except I'm a stranger to myself. I have a life that doesn't feel like it's mine. I can't remember my fantastic kids. I don't know my own wife, the woman who stood by me this far through my rehabilitation.*

Danielle's picture stared back at him, her lovely smile making his soul brighten. As if down deep he did remember, as if she had made him come alive once. He suspected the days before her were colorless in comparison, as if he'd been simply walking through life.

Her face was younger in the picture, softer, untouched by the fine lines of worry his injury had carved there. He would give anything to be able to wipe away that worry. To make things right. She was an amazing woman, and from the moment he'd woken from the coma to see her at his side, he'd been blown away by her.

What kind of wife fought so hard for her husband? Who rarely had left his side during his coma. Who had broken down in tears of gratitude, pressing close in a hug, holding him so tight.

The kind of woman who was true and good and loved deeply, that's who.

How could he not have been awed by her? Even through the pain and fog the coma and accident had made of his brain, it took him all of a second to appreciate how blessed he was to have such a wife.

He turned the page, stopping to listen to the snippet of her soft alto that carried down the hall. She was talking with her sister Rebecca, the one in college, who had arrived to stay with the kids. She was the one who'd missed all their family get-togethers—including church—over the week since he'd come home. Trouble with the boyfriend, Danielle had explained quickly, promising she wouldn't be with her sister for long.

He didn't mind waiting. He was sort of nervous about this date. He wished the sound of her voice could tug at some recognition, but no, nothing. He turned his attention to the page in front of him. It was all done up with pink-and-gold ribbons and lace, and a wedding invitation with a date and their parents' names. The next page was full of personal snapshots someone had taken—maybe Danielle, as the caption read, The Morning of our Wedding.

He glanced at photos of Danielle in her robe, laughing with her sisters. Hugging her mother. Standing in her wedding dress looking so happy. He'd never seen a more beautiful sight.

That was his wife. His throat closed. If she had known what was down the road for her, would she still have married him anyway? Failure beat at him, and he closed the album. Set it on the bedside table. Fighting back the terrible sense he had failed his family. One bullet had changed the course of their lives; he feared that old life—and the old Jonas—were gone for good.

"There. I've got everything squared away. Rebecca broke up with her boyfriend so we had some serious stuff to talk about. Thanks for waiting." Danielle—Dani, as her family called her—swept into the room wearing a knee-length pink dress and it made her look so beautiful that he could not believe his luck.

What a blessing she was. He pushed away his nervousness. Her smile lit him up like hope as she reached for his hand.

"So, do you want to go out to dinner with me, handsome?"

Did he ever. He rose to his feet shakily, wishing he was stronger, the way he used to be—for her. But she didn't seem to mind as he transferred his weight to the walker. "I'm a married man, lady. Not sure what my wife is going to do if I say yes."

When something amused her, little sparkles flashed in her wide brown eyes. "I think she'll allow it this one time. But if you try to make off with any other women, watch out."

"What women? All I can see—will ever be able to see—is you."

"There you go, being charming again." She grabbed her purse—a smaller one than the one she usually dragged around with the kids—and escorted him to the door. "No wonder I fell for you."

When she looked at him like that, as if she knew him to the soul, he had to believe everything would turn out all right. That the Lord would not have brought him this far in vain. He just had to keep working hard and believing.

And getting to know his incredible wife.

There was a young woman settled on the couch reading

a book with brown hair and quiet eyes. She looked up with a shy smile. "Hi, Jonas. You're doing so great."

That was Rebecca, Danielle's baby sister. He was starting to keep all the sisters straight. He took another step forward. "I'm doing okay. Thanks for watching the kids tonight."

"It's my pleasure. Besides, I owe Dani."

Beside him, Danielle shook her head, tugging him gently in the direction of the garage door. "You know that's not true. I'm here anytime for you. Heaven knows you've been there for me, kiddo."

The sisters exchanged emotional looks, as if in silent understanding before Danielle opened the door to the garage. "Becca, Spence will be back with the kids in ten minutes tops. He took them to Mr. Paco's Tacos. He said he'd bring enough food back for you, too."

"That brother of ours. He needs his own family. What are we going to do with him?"

"I don't know. We can't marry him off. No woman in her right mind will have him. Not that we haven't tried to set him up."

"To no avail." A loving joke, apparently, as the sisters nodded knowingly together.

He hated the walker because he had to struggle to use it. It slowed him down. It made him look less…less than able and less than the man he'd been. All right, so he was less these days, and it was a painful reminder, one he didn't need. He could see that enough for himself.

"Call if you have any troubles," Danielle called out, holding the door patiently as he pushed the walker through the door. "I have my cell on."

"You're on a date," Rebecca called out. "No worrying about the kids. I've got things covered here."

"Oh, I know. It's just hard to turn off the mom mode." Danielle laughed at herself, following him into the garage. "Bye!"

Rebecca's answering "bye!" echoed briefly through the doorway before the door clicked shut, leaving him alone with his wife. His stunning, wonderful wife. His heart ached in all the empty places where he supposed his memory and his love for her used to be. He wished he could remember one thing about her, anything, and then maybe he wouldn't feel so formal, as if he were with an acquaintance, someone he only knew distantly, instead of the woman who had given him two fantastic kids.

Everything in his soul longed to love this woman who opened the passenger door for him and did not look at him as less. No, when he gazed into her wide liquid eyes, he could almost see a glimpse of what had been. He could almost see who he'd been.

"Are you hungry?" She smiled up at him as she folded up and stowed the walker.

"Starving. Where are you taking me?" He settled unsteadily into the seat.

"Where we went for our first date." Her smile turned mischievous as she leaned closer to help him with the seat belt buckle. "I know you don't remember, but it's always been our family's favorite. It's the best steak in town."

"Steak? Sounds good. Am I going to need my wallet?"

"It's my treat."

"That doesn't seem very gentle—" He couldn't grasp the word. Polite? Manly? The word hovered just beyond reach and then it slipped into his mind. "It wouldn't be gentlemanly of me, making such a quality lady pay."

"Quality, huh?" Her face softened, and some of the ever-present tension washed from her face. "Jonas, you're the quality one, believe me."

"That can't be." She must not know what he saw when he looked at her. The woman who sat by him so he wouldn't be alone in a coma. The woman who fought with doctors and the insurance and through her own exhaustion to help him with his rehabilitation. The woman who didn't look at him with pity or unease because of his partial paralysis.

Quality was too small a word, as was every other word he could think of to describe her.

"Don't worry about it." Her hand covered his and gently squeezed. Reassuringly. Sweetly. "I may be paying, but I'll use the credit card with your name on it."

"I'd like that." Jonas's empty heart filled with a strange surge of emotion. She deserved his very best, and he was going to make sure he gave it to her.

"What did I like here?"

Danielle looked over the top of her menu at her husband across the table from her. He still looked good in a suit—wait, he looked even better because he was right here with her, when she'd been terrified she would lose him.

Her heart fluttered. She loved this man in more ways than she could count. "Here's where I could cause all sorts of trouble for you, handsome."

His puzzled expression melted into a shy grin. "That means what?"

"Not only do I know what you like, I know what you don't like."

"I'm in a—what does Tyler say?—a pickle. I have to trust you."

"You do. Lucky for you, I won't torture you by having you order the prawns."

"Prawns?" He glanced down at the menu, searching the words and the pictures of the tempting food. He awkwardly tapped one of the pictures with his gnarled hand. "Oh, I see. The prawns."

"Do you remember not liking them?"

"No. I wish I could. I just don't like the look of 'em."

"That's got to be a promising sign, at least." Danielle reached over to touch another picture on the menu. Jonas could read, but she thought the picture might strike an image in his injured brain. "You always order the filet mignon. Medium well. With the salad and the loaded baked potato."

"That sure does look good." He closed the menu. "Why don't I like prawns?"

"Your birthday. A fishing trip to the Oregon Coast. Prawns for lunch and then a boat excursion in choppy seas. How's that for a clue?"

He chuckled, and for an instant he was like the old Jonas, the hint of the man she knew so well. "I used to think it was a blessing you could remember for both of us. Now I'm not so sure. You know all my secrets."

"That was the kind of marriage we had."

"The kind we have." He reached across the table for her hand.

His gesture was so sincere that her heart broke all over again. He didn't know what they'd had. She prayed they could get there again. She missed him, with all the depth of her soul. She missed talking with him, leaning on him, sharing with him, and, most of all, she missed loving him. The weight of his hand on hers, so warm, brought back memories of all the times he had touched her in comfort, in sweetness, in love.

The waitress chose that moment to stop at their table. Jonas, bless him, did not let go.

"Danielle. Jonas." It was Marni, from their church. "How wonderful to see you, Jonas. I don't suppose you remember me."

"No, miss, I'm sorry, I don't."

Danielle watched the puzzlement creep back onto Jonas's face.

"About two years ago, I was coming home from closing up here, I hit a patch of ice and got myself hurt pretty bad. You were on patrol that night and stayed with me until the ambulance came. You even drove my aunt to the hospital to see me and then back home. You took care of the tow call, and when I came home from the hospital, my car was repaired and in my carport. I don't suppose you remember."

"Nope. I'm glad you're better now."

That was her Jonas. Danielle ached with love for him. Such a caring man. Always a man she—and everyone else—had counted on.

Please, remember me, Jonas. It was a wish from her soul. Danielle closed her menu. "Marni brought by a casserole for the family every Saturday afternoon."

"Did she now?" Jonas looked bewildered.

He had no idea all the outpouring of care and prayer that had come his way. What goes around comes around, and the old adage had proved true in his case. So many people had done so much for him and their family.

"It was the least I could do." Marni gave a shrug. "I felt bad for all of you. I prayed so hard for you and Dani."

Danielle's throat tightened. "Marni, it made such a difference. Thank you."

The waitress swiped her eyes. "Goodness, it does my heart good to see you both here tonight. Now, what can I start you off with? Our appetizer platters are on special tonight."

There it was, that incredible healing sense of fellowship and community. Never had she been so aware of it than after Jonas was shot. "Jonas loves the mozzarella sticks. Thank you, Marni, for everything."

"Not a problem." She took their drink and food orders with a smile and sauntered away, leaving a silence behind.

She took solace when he didn't move his hand from hers. They sat in silence, and yet the distance between them felt vast. She hadn't noticed it before, at least not like this. She sat face-to-face with him finally—without the medical staff at the rehab clinic, or the kids to interrupt them, or errands pulling her in one direction and worries tugging her in another.

What did she say now? Conversation had always flowed between them. From their first date, they had just clicked. It had not been like this, uncomfortable, fighting for common ground. What she wanted to talk about, he could not remember. He looked so serious that she didn't want to remind him of what was lost.

Her hand remained in his, and that *did* feel the same, as it once had. His warmth was so alive; he felt so solid and capable. His one touch could open her heart the way nothing in this world could. Why did it feel as if she were sitting with a stranger?

"Jonas!" Mark Whitman, a fellow state trooper and second cousin through Gran's side of the family, came up to the table. "Sorry to interrupt, Dani."

"Not at all. It's good for Jonas to see you."

"Yeah? It's good to see Jonas out and about. We've been missing you in the shop."

"We work together?" Jonas rubbed his temple with his free hand. Was it possible that he was remembering?

"That's right. You were my sergeant. You mostly had a desk job, but now and then, to fill in on vacation, you went out on patrol." Mark hesitated, as if afraid to say too much.

That was why Jonas had pulled over a speeder that fateful night over a year ago. The man had an outstanding warrant, had panicked and shot Jonas without warning. The shooter had left him there, terribly wounded. He'd driven away and had never been caught.

Jonas stopped rubbing his temple and gave Mark a smile. He pulled his hand away from hers to shake his fellow trooper's hand. "Sorry I don't remember you."

"No worries. I just thought I'd come over and let you know we're praying for you and can't wait for you to get back to your desk."

"Thanks, Mark." Jonas looked so pale. "I can't wait, too."

"Dani." Mark gave a nod and went on back to his table far down the aisle.

Heart thumping, she watched Jonas's face carefully. He was rubbing his temple again. Did that mean there was a glimmer of a memory? Something familiar just out of reach? Hope nearly lifted her right off the seat.

"Did he used to be a friend?"

"Yes." There it was: hope. A sign from heaven that her Jonas was coming back to her. She simply had to keep believing. Keep trusting that God would bring them together again. Gratitude filled her and she found it easy to smile. "You and Mark often went to the gym to work out together."

Marni returned to deliver their drinks and platter of mozzarella sticks, hot and crispy.

"I used to *like* to go to the gym?" His lopsided grin was a little straighter, a little more like his old one. "Physical therapy is not fun. I don't like to go now. Maybe that'll change."

"It already is." She felt it all the way to the bottom of her soul.

Danielle navigated the minivan along the country road that swung along the wide banks of the Gallatin River. Dust kicked up behind them like a pleasant haze and leaves from the overarching trees rustled like music. She spotted the park's entrance in a maple grove and pulled into the nearly empty gravel lot. Only a few utility vehicles were parked, awaiting their owners, who were probably serious hikers, judging by the late evening hour.

"This is someplace important." Jonas studied the trail leading into the national forest. "I brought you here on our first date?"

"You did." Danielle turned off the engine and grabbed the keys. The faint scent of dust and pollen hovered in the air as she closed the windows. "Do you remember why?"

When he shook his head, she didn't take that as a bad sign. There was a lot for him to remember, so much water beneath the bridge of their lives. "Are you feeling up to a short walk?"

"Pretty lady, I would walk anywhere with you."

The sunshine on her face felt sweeter as she circled around the minivan to retrieve her husband's walker. Her husband. Nothing felt better than being able to be here, with him, at his side. Joy lifted her up as if she were floating two inches above the ground.

He waited, standing with one hand on the side of the van for support, while she unfolded his walker. "I'm not charming you now."

As he'd done on their first date. "What do you mean? I'm perfectly charmed by you." She set the walker on the ground. "There was a lot I didn't tell you about that night."

"Why didn't you?" His handsome face tightened as he took the walker's grips. How he must hate that thing. She couldn't help laying her hand on the strong curve of his shoulder, not knowing what to say to comfort him.

"Mostly because my family was listening to everything, and this is private, between you and me."

He shuffled the walker forward in the resistive gravel. "You said mostly. Because you want me to remember what happened."

"No." I want you to remember me. Maybe it was selfish, she didn't know, but she had never felt lonelier at her husband's side. Never felt so lost with God's beautiful nature and reassuring sunshine all around her. "My prayers were answered when you woke from your coma. Don't you forget that."

He nodded as if in understanding but the strong line of his jaw hardened. He seemed to disagree with her. They walked in silence; it was easier for him that way. Birds twittered in the high branches, some taking flight at the approach of two suspicious humans in their midst. Others sang on sweetly. Fragrant wild roses tumbled on long canes toward the path. Jonas stopped his walker.

He's remembering. Hope hit her like a powerful wave and left her wobbling, left her dizzy. Did he remember how he'd stopped to pick her a bouquet of the sweet, gentle roses? Did he remember how much she loved their old-world fragrance? Because from the moment he'd given her the flowers, cupping her hand with his and gazing deep into her eyes, she had tumbled so fast and hard in love with him there had been no end to that love, no measure, no condition.

Could it be that he knew? That he was coming back to her?

Chapter Six

Danielle watched her husband study the soft, open-faced roses for a few moments longer.

He gave his walker a push and moved on. "You have bushes like that in the backyard."

Fine, so her hopes were too high. She stayed at his side. "Yes. You planted them for me the spring after we bought the house."

"Did I dig the holes for all the other plants and trees, too?"

"Yes."

"I hope I didn't dig that big hole for the swimming pool. That's a lot of shoveling."

"No, but you offered to, as a joke." They laughed together. How good that felt. It helped chase away her disappointment.

As they reached the footbridge that spanned the ravine and the gurgling creek below, she brushed away the expectation that he would remember. Maybe she was pressuring him without meaning to.

But she remembered how they'd stood in the middle of that span of narrow bridge and talked until sunset. That they'd walked back in the dark to his truck and sat talking in the parking lot for what seemed like a few more minutes, although it had been hours. They'd been hungry to know everything about one another, savoring the rush of emotion that seemed to come alive when they were together, and unable to let the evening end.

How her mom had given her a talking-to when she'd come home at midnight! She hadn't even been aware of the time passing back then.

Now every minute felt like a century.

He was breathing harder by the time they'd made it a third of the way across the bridge. He was tiring. Poor Jonas. "Let's just stand right here at the rail."

"I can't argue with that." He worked so hard to keep his hardships from her, and he was doing it now with a smile in his voice.

She knew, because it was what she did, hiding from him all the ways she was hurting.

"This is a nice place to bring someone on a first date." He was looking around at the lush green foliage and dappled trees and the span of sky showing the snowcapped peaks of the Rocky Mountain Range.

"It was one of your favorite hikes along this trail. You don't remember living down the road, do you? When you first moved to Montana to take a job with the state patrol, you rented a little house about two miles south of here."

"Your grandmother." He lit up with realization. "When I met you. I see now."

"Yes." That was good enough for now. She covered his hand with hers and rubbed a little at his stiff muscles. He didn't stop her. Touching him again dragged up more loneliness from her soul. How could she begin to explain how lonely she was for him? For his kiss, his strength, his shelter?

"Are you disappointed in me?"

"What?" She looked up into his sad eyes. "How can you say that?"

"I can see a lot. How it was when I was in that coma. I can see the—the strain on you. The stress." He tore his gaze away from her, staring out into the peaceful woods. Then down into the gulley where water swirled and bubbled.

He'd seen all that? She broke a little more. Why had their wonderful, perfect lives shattered in the first place? It was not God's doing, she had to remind herself, but a desperate man's decision to shoot a gun—a man with free will.

Her hands stilled, cradling Jonas's. "All of this hasn't been easy for me, it's true. But it's nothing at all, trust me, compared to what you've been through. I only want to make things easier for you."

"That's my job. Not yours. I'm supposed to take care of you."

"And you've done such an amazing job all through our marriage. Can't you see that, too?"

He nodded. "We have a nice home. Comfortable things. We have the kids. They need me to take care of them, too."

How tortured he looked, struggling so hard not to show it. But she could see, now that he was not keeping it hidden so deeply from her. "Then you also know that all the stress and worry and nights in the hospital by your side, I did for you. To take care of you."

"You didn't leave me. Your sisters have said that."

"Of course I stayed with you. Because I love you."

His jaw trembled once—just once. That was her Jonas,

so tough on the outside, so tender inside. "I see how you are. How hard you work to take care of the kids. Of me. You did all that, and for what? For this. For me, now."

She saw the pain stark on his face and felt it in her heart. That was how it had always been between them. "Oh, Jonas. No. Do you think I'm disappointed that you use a walker?"

"That's a nice way of saying I'm disabled. That's what they call me now and it makes you sad." He stood soldier-strong, worrying not for himself, but for her.

She could feel that, too. "No, handsome. That's not why I'm sad. I don't care about those things. You're here. That's what matters to me. That you're right here with me."

"You need a whole man. A strong husband."

"I need you, Jonas. You. No one else. Just the way you are. However you are. Don't you know how proud I am of how hard you worked to beat the coma? To fight to recover as much as you can?"

His throat worked. "I'm fighting hard for you. For the kids."

"I know. I fought hard for you, too, all those long days and nights in the hospital. Can't you see how it was? I wasn't sitting there for my own reasons. I was there for you. So you wouldn't be alone in the dark. So you wouldn't die—if that happened—alone without my hand in yours." Tears burned in her eyes but she could not look away from him until there was understanding in his eyes.

Realization changed his face. His eyes softened with understanding. His hand in hers relaxed, as if this worry had been the reason for his tension. How could he think she was ashamed he wasn't the same? That he was no longer strong? He was the strongest man she'd ever known, especially now. Somehow she had to let him know that.

She took a wobbly breath, hearing the emotion catch like a sob in her throat and did her best to explain. "I never stopped believing in you. Never stopped having faith that you would open your eyes. That's why I stayed, too. So that when you woke up, you were not alone."

"You did all that for me."

"Yes. Don't get me wrong. I didn't want you to leave me. But either way, regardless of what happened, you would have my love."

A muscle ticked in his jaw, but he said nothing. He looked as if he couldn't.

She could feel that, too. His relief. His gladness, which hurt like sorrow. "No matter what, you have my love. Everything I do is for you, Jonas. It's always been that way since the first time we were standing on this bridge all those years ago."

"Is that when you fell in love with me?"

"Yes. On our first date. I've never had a moment of doubt since then. You've never given me a reason to. Especially not now. Do you understand?"

"I do."

Deep with emotion, his voice moved through her like a hymn, strengthening her, but it wasn't enough. *Do you love me?* She ached with the question she was not strong enough to ask. It would put too much pressure on him, she reasoned, to feel what he was supposed to, not what was. And if she were honest with herself, she was too afraid to ask that question. She did not think she could hear the word *no,* even if it were the honest answer and not his fault.

She was still a stranger to him; there was still a lot of distance to bridge between them. But it was a start. They were headed in the right direction, and with his hand in hers, it was clear that they were no longer heart-to-heart. They were not emotionally connected, the way they always used to be.

"You look sad. I do that to you."

"You don't, no." She squeezed his hand with hers. Love bubbled up, ever renewed like the creek below them, always running, always singing. "Thank you for waking up, Jonas. For coming out of that coma. That's what matters."

"No." He studied her with surprising intent. "You want things the way they were. You want a whole man for a husband."

Why couldn't he understand? "Jonas, all I want is for you to love me."

There were the words, tumbling out the way they always used to. She'd always told Jonas everything; as he had done for her. There had been no secrets between them until now. There were very many secrets, all for the right reasons. Words she could not say to save them both pain.

In the silence she hung her head, waiting, just waiting, knowing her Jonas would only speak the truth to her, and knowing that he could not say and feel what she needed.

He broke the silence. "I was looking at the wedding pictures. We were happy."

"One of the top three best days of my life."

"The other two. When Tyler and Madison were born?" His question was more than the fact that he didn't remember those days, much more. It meant that he was starting to know her, just a little.

Memories warmed her. "At midnight on the eve of our

wedding there was a knock at my bedroom window. Nearly scared the stuffing out of me. I pulled back the curtain and there you were, grinning through the glass at me standing in the middle of the shrubbery."

He chuckled. "I did that?"

"Yes you did, handsome, and with a handful of flowers. When I opened the window, you told me that you'd come for a kiss, since it was officially our wedding day."

"Did you kiss me?"

"After I whacked you with my pillow. We were laughing as we kissed, and then you left me. I had the sweetest dreams that night. I wanted to marry you so much."

"I know that from the pictures. I also know that I was feeling the same way. We both looked happy."

"We were." Beautifully happy. It wasn't right what happened. Jonas did not deserve what happened to him. And now they were left with pieces of that beauty and bits of their love.

"We will be again," he promised. "I'll make sure of it."

The sun chose that moment to cast its last light on their world, calm and golden and translucent: the exact color of hope.

Danielle was in the hallway, closing the garage door behind them, when she heard Madison's sleepy voice call out from her bedroom. "Daddy! Kiss-kiss!"

"Lucky you." It felt great to see how pleased Jonas looked that his daughter wanted him. Another thing almost back to normal. She touched his elbow. "Go on. No doubt Tyler is watching for you, too. I want to talk with Rebecca for a few minutes, then I'll be along."

"Okay." Jonas's step was almost chipper as he manhandled the walker down the hallway.

Memories clung to her like the shadows. Images of before Jonas had been shot, barreling down the hallway to scoop Tyler up into a hug. Or with Madison on his shoulders squealing with delight. Of Jonas quietly checking on the sleeping children, adoration shining off him as he carefully shut one door and then the other. Of how he would turn to her, smile and wink at her. That they could be alone once the kids were asleep.

She watched Jonas disappear through Madison's doorway. He didn't look back at her. He didn't wink or look forward to their alone time after putting the kids to sleep. Tears scored the back of her eyes and she blinked them away. The empty hallway stared back at her, and she heard Madison's faint giggle. She smiled, brushing away the sting from her eyes. She just wanted their lives put back together again.

It would take time, that's all. Madison's giggle floated down the hall, and it warmed her. She steeled herself, clung to the hope she'd felt on the bridge as the sun had set on them. She headed through the kitchen to the dining room.

Rebecca looked up from packing her tote. "That Madison. All the cutie did was get out of bed and keep asking where you two were."

"At least she's over her fears. When Jonas came home I was afraid she wouldn't be close to him again." Danielle pulled out a chair and collapsed into it. Since it felt good just to sit there, she had to conclude that she was more tired than she'd thought. "How are things going with you?"

"Oh, just hunky-dory, thankyouverymuch." Rebecca

kept packing one thick textbook after another into her backpack. She had a big smile on her face but shadows of pain in her eyes. The breakup with Chris had been hard on her. "Ava came by earlier with some cookies for the kids. Katherine called a few minutes ago just to chat. She wants you to call her back when you can. I think she wants the scoop on how tonight went. Oh, and Spence dropped by for the bookstore's financial statements."

Danielle groaned. How could she have forgotten? She did the monthly accounting for the family's Christian bookstore. The extra income had helped out a lot with all of the extra medical bills. "I've got to get cracking on the general ledger. I'm stuck."

"If you tell Spence that, he isn't going to be too happy. He's coming over tomorrow to mow the lawn. Maybe you'll be unstuck by then."

Something else to hope for. "It's Friday night. Spence should be out on a date, finding himself a wife, instead of home worrying about his work."

"He's lonely, I think that's why he's so harsh. He works so hard at the store. You know he does. He's shorthanded and wanted me to work, but I told him I'm already putting in long hours at the church. I felt bad that I can't help him."

One look at Rebecca's sweet face, and Danielle knew her baby sister needed a little reassurance. "Spence understands that. He's just stressed."

"He is." Rebecca sighed as she zipped her backpack, perhaps keeping the conversation on their brother to keep it off of herself. "Ava thinks we should try to fix him up again. What do you think?"

"I think Spence definitely needs help, but he's a grown

man. He can find a woman to date if he wants to." She didn't add that as much as she worried about Spence's happiness, she was more concerned with Rebecca's. She spotted the pink bakery box on the counter. "Let's have some cookies."

"Let me." Rebecca headed to the kitchen, faster in her tennis shoes.

Danielle followed her, tapping in her low heels. "What are you doing? I'll get my own cookie."

"I don't mind." Rebecca brought the small box to the table and flipped open the lid. "Did you and Jonas have a nice evening?"

"We did." It hadn't gone as she'd hoped, but she was starting to see something else, too. Something she didn't want to look at. Although their first date had gone well, Jonas was still a stranger to her and to himself.

Not what she'd expected. She'd truly believed tonight would spark some locked-up memory. She felt oddly alone as she chose a cookie in the shape of a ballerina bear and studied Ava's workmanship. Pink icing ballet tutu and shoes, a glittery crown studded with golden sugar and a cute smiling bear face. She nibbled on a toe. "Time to talk about you some more. Breakups are hard. Are you all right?"

Rebecca, always quiet, seemed to withdraw a little, as she tended to do. She didn't answer right away, which was telling, too. She chose a spotted dog cookie. "Oh, you know. I guess things had been heading this way for a while so it wasn't exactly a surprise to me. But I'm fine."

Which meant, not so fine. Danielle wished she could make Rebecca see that this was for the best. "It's never fine when dreams die. It hurts."

Rebecca took another nibble on her cookie and nodded. "This, too, shall pass, right? I don't want you worrying about me, Dani. I've decided to adopt Ava's view of things."

"Oh, no, that's trouble."

"Remember when she went on a no-date policy? Well, that's going to be me. I need a serious break from all things male. I've got a lot on my plate anyway."

"If I remember right, as soon as Ava instituted her no-date policy, she met Brice. Her Mr. Right."

"Well, I'm pretty sure I don't have one of those waiting in the wings somewhere." Rebecca slid her backpack strap over her shoulder and dug for her car keys. "I never want to feel this way again."

Uh-oh. There was more going on than her sister was admitting to. Danielle wished she could pry it out of Rebecca, but she was already leaving and quietly pulling away. "Love doesn't hurt like that when it's right."

"Love hurts. I've watched you this last year, hurting terribly, Dani. It seems to me it hurts either way. If you let someone close, you can lose them. If you let someone close, they might hurt you. It's a pickle."

There was that word again. "It's definitely a journey, but it's one I'm glad I made."

"Well, maybe I'll feel differently in a while." Already Rebecca was heading through the kitchen, car keys and cookie in hand. "Let me know if you need me next week. I know with Aubrey's wedding coming up, everyone's too busy to stay with the munchkins the way they used to. I have more time now that Chris is gone. I don't mind coming over."

"I'll take you up on that." Danielle gave her sister a hug.

"You drive safe. Give me a quick jingle so I know you got home okay."

"You two have been apart a long time. You don't need me interrupting your evening. I'll make it home just fine, don't you worry."

Danielle watched until her sister crossed the lawn and circled around to her little red car parked along the street. The engine purred to life and headlights blazed on, and after a final wave, Danielle closed and locked the door. As unhappy as Rebecca was, surely better things were right around the corner for her.

As she went around tidying up the kitchen and getting ready for the morning, she listened to the low murmur of voices floating serenely down the hall. Jonas must have gotten Madison settled, and now was in Tyler's room.

Which is where she found him when she headed down the hall. Sure enough, Jonas was on the edge of Tyler's bed, talking quietly with him. The little boy with the sleep-tousled hair and fireman pajamas gazed with total adoration at his daddy.

"We'll have to ask your mom about that," Jonas was saying with a touch of humor in his rich baritone. "I'm not sure this is the right time."

"Having a dog is always right." Tyler, so earnest, popped off his pillow to wrap his arms around his dad's chest. "I really love the dotted kind. The ones on the fire trucks."

A Dalmatian, Danielle realized. Tyler had been pestering her for a dog ever since he'd met his uncle Brice's retriever. Rex had more heart than sense, which made him the perfect dog, in Danielle's opinion. But with Jonas injured and battling with his rehabilitation in costly big-city facilities, there hadn't been the extra finances or time to spend with a puppy.

"But Mommy said when you came home we could get one." Tyler, all hope, kept a careful watch on his dad's face. "I want one *real* bad."

Jonas ran his hand over the crown of his son's head, gentle and loving as always. "I'm sure you do."

There was her Jonas, not so far away at all. She thought of all the times he had sat right there on the edge of their son's bed and chatted with him, a devoted father. For once, the memories of the past and the image of the present were one and the same.

Jonas turned toward her, sensing her in the doorway, and the look he sent her was as telling as any words could be.

Your turn now, sweetheart.

She laughed, stepping into the room. "Tyler, we'll talk about that tomorrow."

"But, Mom! You could say yes right now." Knowing he was a cutie and that he had her wrapped around his little finger, Tyler gave her a sweet, expectant grin.

Danielle sighed. It was hard being a mom. "Tomorrow. I mean it. Right now, you are supposed to be asleep, tiger."

"I know." Tyler flopped back into his pillow. "But I would sleep best if I had my own dog."

"Who wouldn't?" Jonas winked as he struggled to his feet. "We'll talk about it tomorrow. Good night, son."

"'Night, Dad." Tyler looked bursting with happiness, so glad to have his daddy back in his daily life—and that promise of a dog much closer now.

Danielle was glad, too. She bent to kiss her little boy's brow and wish him sweet dreams. When she turned around,

Jonas was watching her from the doorway, his eyes dark with unreadable emotion.

Please let it be love for me, she wished with all of her heart. Her love for Jonas drew her to him like a hook pulling her forward. He turned out the light, she closed the door, and they headed down the hall together.

The door to their room stood open, the lights off, dark and quiet. She felt a tingle of anticipation wash over her. She was going to be alone with her husband, her beloved Jonas. Finally. Tonight he wasn't too tired from a demanding physical therapy appointment—there hadn't been one.

Tonight she needed the shelter of his arms. The loving sweetness of being with him, wrapped up in the blessing of their tenderness for one another. She needed him. She was not whole, not complete without his love.

She turned on the bedside lamp, a soft light that cast a glow through the darkness. Her stomach fluttered with a touch of nerves. It had been so long. She loved him so much. He ambled across the room and stopped, his gaze finding hers. She felt her soul sigh with recognition. Re-enacting their first date may not have sparked any memories for him, but she believed it had helped his heart to remember hers.

"It's getting late," he said, plainly, simply, as if he were tired.

She watched, her hopes falling, as he and his walker thumped into their bathroom and closed the door.

So, I was wrong. She eased onto the side of the bed. Disappointment splashed through her like a bucketful of cold water. She sat shivering, as if she were as cold on the outside as she was down deep. She knew they had made progress together tonight as man and wife, but the distance between them was still so great. Not even that distance could stop her from loving him. What she would give for just one kiss.

With a sigh, she turned down the bed, took off the pillow shams and set the morning's alarm.

Chapter Seven

All I want is for you to love me. Danielle's confession troubled Jonas all the week through. It whispered to him every morning when he opened his eyes and saw how hard she worked for him and the kids, and always with a smile on her lovely face. It drove him through his painful, grueling physical therapy appointments where he went beyond what the therapist asked him to do.

Her words ate at him in all the dozens of silent moments between them through the day—when they were in the car driving from one appointment to the next. When they were in the house together, she in one room, he in another. When they were at the table, quiet as their children talked and giggled.

It tore him up every time he looked at her. Especially now when she walked into the living room wearing the dark blue dress that shimmered around her. His jaw dropped. The photo album he held ruffled shut. No woman on this planet could ever be as lovely as his wife.

Yes, the Lord had blessed him infinitely.

"Do I look all right?" She looked nervous of his opinion and patted at the sleek cinnamon shine of her hair. "I hope no one can tell I threw this on in exactly three and a half minutes. This is Aubrey's wedding. I can't have her regretting that she invited me."

"You don't look all r-right." Emotion jammed in his throat. "Y-you look perfect."

For once a smile brightened her face, her eyes, her soul. Jonas stared at her, this lovely creature, and realized it was his words that had made her so happy. Happy like in the pictures he'd studied every spare minute he had. Happy like in the wedding pictures.

And not sad.

"Jonas, there you go, trying to charm me again." She was blushing though, and he realized, as she went to grab her purse from the hallway table, that she was self-conscious. She might not know what he saw: all her beauty, all her strength, all her goodness.

He had to learn her vulnerabilities, too. He could see that.

"I'll grab the kids' things and be right back," she said adorably. "Then we can go."

"Daddy! Daddy!" Madison stormed up to him in a pair of her mother's too-big shoes and held out a plastic phone to him. "It's ringing!"

He'd quickly learned a lot about his daughter. She loved pink and purple. Her favorite toy was the play cell phone she talked into constantly. She went from being a ballerina to a princess to a mermaid all in one afternoon. But his wife, she wasn't so easy to peg. As he leaned to put his ear to the phone, he kept his eye on her. He couldn't rightly say why his heart stirred, but it did.

"Hello?" He gave his daughter a grin. "Maddy, it's for you."

"For me? Goody!" Pleased, the little girl took back the phone, chattering away as if to a good friend.

He had no trouble at all knowing where Madison had learned such a thing. She had watched her mom and her aunts always talking to one another.

She needs a sister of her own, he thought, and when he glanced at his wife, he couldn't help blushing.

She was no longer a stranger to him, no longer someone he didn't know. He had learned a lot on their date. That the Lord had blessed him with a great woman, a woman he must have once loved beyond his own life.

He had learned from the wedding album, which he had studied three times now, that they had been best friends, best everything, just as Danielle had once said. He didn't know what that all meant, but he had a pretty good idea whenever he saw his wife looking so sad and alone and strong.

He had been her pillar. He could see that, too. He stared down at his gnarled hand and the cane, for which he had just traded his walker. No, he was hardly strong enough for her to lean on.

But he would be.

"Hey, Dad!" Tyler burst through the slider door, his good clothes spotted with water from a quick trip outside to the backyard. "I turned off the hose like you said!"

"You got yourself a little wet there, son."

"I know. There was a hot spot I'd forgotten to put out! I couldn't leave it." A devoted play fireman, Tyler raced across the room, his church shoes squishing. "But do you know what?"

"What?"

"If I had a dog, then he coulda helped me."

"I get the hint, buddy." Jonas thought of the vacation pictures from the first album he'd studied, and how his son had been at his side in nearly every photo. Of the way Tyler gazed up at him with such love and need.

He felt that way about his little boy—he loved and needed him, too. He ruffled Tyler's downy brown hair. "Your mom promised we would start looking into getting a dog after the wedding."

"Good thing Aunt Aubrey is getting married *today* cuz I can't wait anymore!" Good-natured, Tyler rolled his eyes, and plopped on the couch. "Know what?"

"What?" Jonas raised his arm so Tyler could lean close against him. It was a rare kind of sweetness when his son snuggled close.

"I'm gonna name him Lucky."

"That's a mighty good name."

"Cuz he's gonna be a mighty good dog."

Emotion welled up in his chest, making it hard to breathe. Every beat of his heart hurt. Jonas gazed down at the little boy and turned back the pages of the photo album he had taken off Danielle's bookcase. The picture was of a red-faced, hours-old newborn, swaddled in blue, napping in a hospital bassinet. The tag overhead read, Baby Boy Lowell.

"That's me." Tyler leaned close to study the page of pictures. "I was real little then. Maddy was like that when we first got her from God at the hospital. She was reaaally little but reaaally loud."

It was a marvel, this baby who had grown into this little boy. Lost memories—lost moments—Jonas could not get back.

"Sorta like now." Tyler grinned, showing off his dimples, nodding to his little sister standing in the middle of the room, talking away at full speed.

"Yip, call me. See yew later, alligator." She disconnected with a flourish. "Mommy!"

Sure enough, Danielle had swept back into the room. Jonas felt his pulse skid to a stop. Everything within him silenced. There were so many memories he'd lost of her, too. So many moments, huge and small. But there, in the album on his knees, was the image he could not remember. Exhausted, pale, happy Danielle propped up in the hospital bed, cradling their son. The woman who had given him a home, and a family—everything that mattered.

"Madison! We're running late. Where are your shoes?"

"I donno." Madison pressed a button and the cell phone rang. "Oop! I gotta take it."

"You can talk while we race, bubbles." Danielle scooped the girl up and settled her onto her hip, still managing to look amazing.

Simply amazing. He could not look away. His eyes refused to move. He wasn't sure his lungs were pulling in air.

"Jonas, are you and Tyler ready? Tyler! Look at you." Danielle shook her head, scattering her chestnut curls. "Well, you're not wet *clear* through. I suppose Aubrey won't mind if her ring bearer is water spotted."

Jonas closed the photo album and set it on the table. "Maybe we can strap him to the top of the minivan. He'll be dry by the time we make it to the church."

"Good idea." Danielle's eyes twinkled merrily at him over the top of Madison's curls.

His heartbeat stalled. Sharing a smile made him feel closer to her. His worries felt lighter as he followed his wife and kids through the house to the garage. Danielle was busy strapping Madison into her seat.

"Noooo! I don' wanna!" the little girl shouted at the top of her lungs, her cell phone clutched in one chubby hand.

"She's still reaaally loud." Tyler climbed into the backseat beside her. "C'mon, Maddy. I have to get buckled in, too."

"But I want Daddy."

Jonas eased in beside his wife and leaned his cane against the open door. "Let me finish buckling her."

"Thank you." She laid her hand on his arm and squeezed once.

Madison's squeals faded away and the heat of the garage with it. His troubles and worries vanished, leaving only a quiver in his heart and an emotion too tender to name. He longed for this moment to last so that he could touch the silken sleekness of her hair and breathe in the fragrance of vanilla and roses. He ached to reach out and draw her into the shelter of his arms.

Then she released him, tapping away in her matching blue shoes to heft the bag for the kids into the back of the van. The moment was broken; his pulse thudded to life again, his troubles returned, and Madison was still fighting her nemesis, the seat belt.

With a final click, she was secure and safe and unhappy. "I wanna sit with you, Daddy."

"I want that, too, princess, but your mom is making me sit up with her."

"Oh." With a gulp, Madison quieted.

Before she could ask the inevitable why question, he hit the button on her cell phone. It rang with a cheerful electronic tune. "You'd better answer that. It could be your aunt."

"Yip." She smiled up at him angelically. "Hello?"

He shut the door and leaned on his cane the few feet to climb up into the passenger seat. His leg was wobbly and hurting him, but he couldn't let Danielle know.

"And you said he could get a dog." She winked at him as she settled behind the wheel. "As if we don't have our hands full enough already."

"Not full enough for me." He winked at her, hoping he was being charming.

Must have worked because she laughed, gentle and warm, and the sound of her laughter made his world brighter. Better.

He clicked his seat belt buckle into place, bowed his head and sent a prayer heavenward as the van rolled out of the garage. *Show me the way, Lord. Show me how to care best for these incredible blessings You have put into my life.*

The van came to a stop, he opened his eyes.

"Please hit the remote for me, handsome." Across the console, she was watching him with soft tenderness on her face.

Tenderness for him.

Yep, he was sure grateful for that. He reached up and hit the button, the garage door slid down and they were off, a family, rolling down the residential street together, awash in sunshine.

With Madison on her hip, Danielle peered through the arched doorway into the church's sanctuary. A string quartet played, while the last of the guests were seated. White roses filled the church in fragrant, pure displays at the end of every aisle, and graced the altar where Aubrey's William was waiting to marry her.

It was hard not to remember her own wedding, pink roses instead of white. She would never forget seeing Jonas standing at that altar, watching for her, and how his face had lit with awe when he saw her for the first time. The dress, she remembered, had been beautiful. She had it still, wrapped carefully and stored in case Madison should ever wish to wear it.

Jonas. There he was, sitting in the second row next to Spence. Marin Baylor, the church's youth pastor and a family friend, was talking with both men. Jonas was smiling—how handsome he looked in his navy-blue suit— but there was nothing except polite interest on his face. Not a single drop of recognition.

"Dani?" Katherine touched her shoulder. "We're ready to start. Is our flower girl ready?"

"She is. You look incredible." She shifted Madison and lowered her gently to the floor, careful not to muss her champagne-colored gown. "Pregnancy agrees with you."

"You have no idea the panic at the final fitting when I didn't fit into this grown, but the owner managed to alter it just enough." Katherine was the epitome of happiness as she took Madison's little hand. "Come with me, princess, okay?"

"'Kay." Madison tilted her head back, her silken curls tumbling around her adorable face. "Bye, Mommy!"

"Bye, baby. I'll be waiting for you at the end of the aisle, okay?"

"Yip." A seasoned flower girl after walking the aisle for

now three of her five aunts, she happily trotted along with Katherine to where Tyler was. He looked like a little man in his black suit, now thankfully dry and in the watchful care of Ava.

"Go be with Jonas," Ava assured her as she knelt to straighten Tyler's bow tie.

That was her family, always reaching out to her, always helping to lighten her load. There was no way she could have gotten through Jonas's coma and rehabilitation without them. They stepped up and looked after the kids, her house, ran errands, kept things together so she could be with her husband. And they were still doing it. Gratitude left her speechless as she looked up to see Spence holding out his hand to her.

"Jonas needs you." No smile, but that was Spence. He was not a happy soul. "People keep coming up to him, and he's having a tough time with it. Hasn't said a word about it, but even I can tell."

So many people he didn't know, folks he had helped out in his job in times of crisis, people he knew from his volunteer work and his active role in the church. All strangers to him now. She could see the strain on his face, the deep-set lines and how pale he looked, how lost.

As she let Spence guide her down the far aisle past so many friendly faces, it was Jonas's need she felt. Jonas's worry. Jonas's fear.

He was afraid he would never remember, too.

"He's looking good." Marin stopped in the aisle as they passed. "Isn't God great?"

"Very."

Marin's words seemed to follow her the few short yards

to the end of the pew where Jonas waited for her. The anxious look on his face eased when she slid onto the bench beside him. She was hardly aware of Spence scooting in on her other side, because Jonas took her hand in his and held on tightly. Relief eased his tense shoulders. Her hopes fluttered when he fit his fingers between hers, just as he always used to do.

"Our wedding was like this." He leaned close to whisper in her ear, just as he used to do, too. Making it somehow feel as if they were all alone. "With our family and friends. I can see what the pictures didn't show."

"What?" She was hardly aware of the music changing or the rustling of the full church turning to watch the central aisle. To her, there was only Jonas.

"All the happiness in the air. How happy everyone must have been for us. How happy I must have been." His gaze was tender as he spoke. "You were beautiful in those pictures. I think maybe more beautiful than the pictures could show. Just like you are now. No picture could be as good as seeing you with my own eyes."

She was no beauty; she knew that. But to hear that her husband thought her so made her throat ache with more emotion than she could measure.

"Look. Maddy." Jonas seemed so proud as he gazed on his daughter, who was a vision in silk and lace, joyfully tossing handfuls of white roses into the air, and then stopping to watch them fall like grace. With a grin on her button face and pleased that she had everyone's attention in the room, she waltzed a few steps forward and repeated the process. Adoring comments floated through the sanctuary.

"That's our little girl," Jonas whispered to her. "Ours."

She heard what he didn't say. She felt it with every fiber of her being. Their marriage, their kids, their family. All had been built on the rock of their love.

She felt a touch at her other elbow. Spence leaned close. "I see someone who just came in. She's in the back."

He was gone, his ominous tone making her worry just a little. Who was this woman? She barely had time to glance over her shoulder; Spence was speaking with someone quietly, blocking her view.

Since Madison was almost out of flowers and nearly at the altar, Danielle regretfully withdrew her hand from her husband's. With his smile in her heart, she went around to sweep Madison into her arms and out of the way of the coming bridesmaids and Tyler, carrying the ring pillow. Looking so handsome, he grinned at her. And resembled his father so very much.

God is great; she knew that of course, but Marin's words had nudged her in a direction she had been already heading anyway.

With her daughter on her hip, she carried Madison past Gran, who waved; past Mom, who blew two kisses, one for each of her girls; past Katherine's and Ava's husbands, who both winked at the little princess. Madison preened sweetly the entire way.

When Danielle slid into place next to her husband, he reached for their daughter and took her onto his knee. Over the top of Madison's frothy curls and gleaming tiara, there was no mistaking the joy in his eyes.

Maybe he was coming to the same conclusions, too. God had graciously answered her prayers. The good Lord had brought Jonas back to her; maybe not whole as he was.

Maybe not the same man he was, but he was here. She had her husband. The children had their father. It was time to let go of her own wants and wishes. She wanted Jonas, her best friend and soul mate back.

Maybe it was time to accept that it might not happen, just as the doctors had said.

The past was gone, whether Jonas remembered it or not. It was behind them. It could never be resurrected. And if his memories of their past never returned, that did not change the course of their lives, of their family, of their commitment to one another. As long as Jonas was here, un-wavering in his promises, that was what mattered. Now mattered. This day, this hour, this moment.

She would have to let go of the rest and be grateful, so infinitely grateful, for what they did have.

When Aubrey appeared at the top of the aisle, Danielle scooped Madison into her arms and stood, holding out her hand to help Jonas. But he did not accept her help. He struggled to stand, gallantly and without his cane, and when he was on his feet and steady, only then did he take her hand. His touch was steadfast and rock solid, making her love him even more.

The reception at Gran's country house was for family only. There had been a larger one after the service at the church in town, for their church family and friends. So it was late, nearly twilight, by the time Danielle did her share of cleanup in the kitchen and went in search of her husband.

Spence, who had promised to stay close to him, had told her Jonas had wanted to sit on the front porch. Mom, who always had the best instincts, decided at that moment to take charge of Madison, who was yawning and getting a little cranky. She'd also promised to keep an eye on Tyler, who was inseparable from Ava and Brice's golden retriever.

As she followed the wraparound porch along the side to the front of the house, she caught sight of Katherine and her stepdaughter, Hayden, doing the last of the hand washables at the kitchen sink. She breathed in the scent of the first bloom of roses clinging to the rails, and realized she was at peace. The worries and hurt that had plagued her had slid away.

No doubt they would be replaced by other ones, since that was the way life always seemed to go, but for now, she felt light as air. Then she turned the corner and saw her husband in the bench swing, staring out at the beautiful mountain range.

"Hey, handsome. Mind if I join you?"

He didn't startle; he must have heard her coming. "I've been saving a place for you."

"Lucky me."

"We're going to have to get Tyler a dog."

"I know." It wasn't the best timing, she thought as she joined her husband, but Tyler had waited long enough. "He's hung on to poor Rex all evening long. It's going to break his heart when we leave."

"Rex's or Tyler's?" Jonas teased.

They smiled together. "That's one of the things I love about you most. Your sense of humor."

"Not my dashing good looks?"

"I don't think you're good-looking, but a girl can't have everything," she quipped, barely able to keep from laughing because it was so far from the truth.

That made him laugh, too, deep and rumbling, a sound of warm joy. He shook his head. "I asked for that one."

"Yes, you did, handsome. Want to tell me why you're out here all by your lonesome?"

"I'm just a little tired."

There was more; she knew it by the lines on his face and the silence that settled like the evening between them. "It has to be hard for you being with all these people who know you."

He looked surprised that she had guessed what he was feeling. "When we've gone to church before, we came late, stayed in the back, left with the last hymn still going."

"Because you had a hard time in a crowd." She understood what was making the lines of misery on his face, of what seemed to weigh heavily on his shoulders. "No one got the chance to really come up to you and talk to you before, unlike now. Spence said when I was in the back of the church with my sisters, that you had a few people talk to you."

"More than a few."

"And you didn't know who they were."

He nodded, his mouth worked, and he turned away, staring hard at a red-tailed hawk circling above the neighbor's far fields. "One was the pastor. I guess she's friends with us?"

"Yes."

"And there were more. People I knew from some committee. From a Bible study. From all kinds of things. I couldn't keep track." His throat worked, as if he were struggling with his emotions. "There's a lot I don't know. I will never know, unless you tell me."

"I'll tell you, Jonas. Anything you want to know."

"Did we have a family party here, too?"

"Yes."

"And did we head off on our honeymoon in a limousine the way Aubrey and William did?"

"Yes. We went to Hawaii. We stayed on Maui in a posh resort. You splurged for a wonderful trip for us."

"I did." He nodded once, as if not at all surprised. "I know why. I wanted to give you a time to remember. Something real nice for my amazing wife."

"You said something like that to me at the time. It was a surprise, where we were going. You refused to tell me. You had Katherine pack my suitcases, so I didn't even know if we were heading off to warm weather or cold. You were bursting with the secret, but when we went to board the Hawaii-bound plane, it sort of gave it away."

"Were you happy?"

"Very. We were there three whole weeks."

"Were you happy?" he asked.

"Very."

"Good to know." He turned toward her and laid his arm along the back of the top rail, not exactly hugging her, but close enough.

Just as he'd done on their second date. Always a gentleman, that was her Jonas. Why hadn't she realized it before? Was he trying to get to know her again? She leaned back, luxuriating in just being with him. "We went snorkeling, surfing and sightseeing, too. We went on a helicopter ride and on catamarans."

"You went snorkeling?"

"Yes, don't look so amused. I know how to swim. We have a pool in our backyard, right?"

"Sure, but you look so...dainty."

"I have pictures, buster. I'll show them to you."

"That's a promise I'm going to make you keep. I want to see you underwater with fish and crawly creatures."

"Now, I didn't say I liked snorkeling, just that I went with you."

"Did I like snorkeling?" He leaned a little closer to her.

It felt as if they were more than just physically closer. She ached with happiness from being so near to him. "That's an answer that will have to wait for the pictures."

"I'll take you to lunch after my physical therapy appointment on Monday. Is it a d-date?" His voice wobbled on that last word.

Tears scalded the back of her eyes. She swallowed hard, to push them away, but his dear face was a little blurry. "It's a date, handsome."

His gaze caressed her face as if seeing her for the first time, as if treasuring every detail. She felt so exposed; this felt so intimate.

Footsteps rang on the porch boards behind them, pounding closer. It was Tyler, coming to find them. The moment was lost, but not the promise.

Chapter Eight

Sunday had been a wild and woolly one, especially with getting everyone ready and in the van for church. There had been Sunday school and the service, then an impromptu chat in the parking lot with the family, which had stretched into a long discussion of the latest on Aubrey and William. When Tyler couldn't stand still a moment longer, the family gathering broke up. There had been lunch out at family favorite Mr. Paco's Tacos, always an adventure with two small children.

Once they reached home, the pace hadn't slowed down any. While Jonas had gone to their room to take a nap, she'd gotten both kids changed, Madison down for her nap, and got Tyler set up in the backyard with his fireman boots and hat. Even as she sat down at her computer in the spare room in the daylight basement, she kept an eye on her son, who hosed down an imaginary fire in the petunia beds. Somehow, she had to finish last month's books for the store before it was time to fix dinner. No problem, right?

Wrong. She'd watched the hands of the wall clock tick

by for more than an hour, without a lot of progress on the troubled general ledger. Her back hurt from sitting so long in the secondhand chair, and she stretched, turning her attention away from the stack of invoices.

She was rewarded with a view of the backyard, where sunshine spilled through the glass. Tyler, drenched from head to boot toe, was now very diligently spraying the lawn with the garden hose, as if it had only been engulfed with a wildfire moments before.

Get back to work, Danielle, she told herself. She flipped the invoice over and started typing. When she glanced over the top of the monitor, Tyler was nowhere in sight. Expecting him to come back into view any moment, she turned to the next document and typed away.

Still no Tyler. But those were his footsteps pounding down the hallway.

"Mom! Hey, Mom! Did you see me put out that fire? Grass fires are the hardest. They can burn for miles and miles in the wild."

"I've heard that, tiger." Since he'd been the one to tell her. She stopped typing. Seeing him burst into the room, dripping and happy and with all his little-boy energy, simply filled her with endless love.

He clutched a handful of wild pink roses and held them out to her, along with a piece of paper. "Here. Dad said I had to give this to you, too, but it's kinda wet."

Wet was an understatement. She took the fragrant, delicate blossoms and the slip of paper he held out to her. "Thank you, baby."

A devoted fireman headed back to the front line, he was

already gone, calling out, "Bye," his boots echoing down the hallway.

Roses. Jonas had remembered. The floral scent tickled her nose and her memories, brought her back to standing on the bridge with her husband in the hopeful light of sunset.

Since the small piece of paper was folded in two, she brushed it open. There was a message, in strange, wobbly handwriting. *Looking forward to our date.*

Jonas.

She knew he was there before the pad of his gait on the carpeted entrance, before the faint clink of his cane, and before she refolded the paper to see him watching her with a question. Her spirit turned toward him like a star faced the earth's pole, for he had always been her center, her anchor, her guiding light.

"Me, too," she told him, his note clutched in her hand. She was breathless as he came toward her. She was captivated, unable to move, as he knelt down before her.

"Do you like the flowers?" he asked.

But he was inquiring about more than the flowers, she knew. "You don't remember giving me these roses after our first date, but you brought me a bouquet anyway."

"Seemed the gentlemanly thing to do."

That was her Jonas, always a gentleman. She stared down at the bouquet picked from the bushes outside, from the bushes Jonas had planted for her as a surprise after Tyler was born. A sign of his devotion to her, he had said at the time. She had to stop herself from wishing that he could remember.

"Your mom is going to watch Madison and Tyler tomorrow. She told me a few things."

"I'm afraid to ask what."

"You should be very afraid." Humor brightened him. "I'll pick you up tomorrow at eleven-thirty sharp."

She loved that he still had his sense of humor intact. The bullet had not taken everything. "I'll see you in the physical therapist's waiting room at eleven-thirty."

"Lucky me." It was not humor that darkened his eyes as he leaned close to press a kiss to her cheek, but it made her laugh all the same.

"No, lucky me," she said, wondering if, somehow, her Jonas was on his way back to her.

The waiting room was busy when Danielle's cell phone rang. She put down her pen, checked the screen and her heart lit up. "Hi, Mom."

"Baby, I have someone here who wants to talk to you." Dorrie sounded happy; she loved taking her granddaughter to swimming class. "Hold on."

Danielle closed her checkbook, the enormous pile of unpaid bills forgotten. There was a shuffle and Madison's singsong voice chattering in the background, and then suddenly, filling her ear.

"Mommy! I swimmed on my own!"

"That's great, bubbles. You are such a good girl."

"I know." Madison had no problem with underconfidence. "Now I get minty cream."

Peppermint ice cream. Danielle could only hope Mom would know what that meant when they got to the ice cream shop. "You be sure and point it out to Grammy, so she knows."

Jonas. She looked up to find him watching her. How

long had he been standing in the middle of the waiting room, pinning her with his intense gaze? Everything within her stilled. He might be leaning heavily on his cane, and he was trying to mask the pain on his face, but he was here. He was hers.

"Madison, do you want your daddy?"

"Yiiiip." Excitement drew out that one word.

"Hold on, cutie." Danielle stood, taking the phone to her husband. "There's a pretty brunette who wants to talk to you."

"There isn't a problem?" One eyebrow crooked up into a question.

"No. Mom's going to keep her for lunch and drop her by after our lunch date."

"Good. I worried something had changed." Jonas took the cell from her, his warm strong fingers brushing hers as she released the phone. His gaze never left her face. "Hi, sweetheart. Did you have fun swimming?"

Jonas loved his children. It was on his face, in his voice, gentle and unbreakable. That was something the bullet hadn't taken. Danielle hiked her purse strap onto her shoulder, remembering the day he'd come out of his coma. Not fully awake and his thoughts confused, as if the coma were trying to pull him back in. He'd stared up at her without a hint of recognition.

Now, when he gazed at her, his eyes were full of gentleness.

"Okay. Bye-bye, Madison." He closed the phone, and he looked steady. Stalwart. Invincible. "Whew, she's cute but she's a talker."

"I can't imagine where she gets it." She took the phone

he offered and slipped it into the outside pocket of her purse. "I never talk on the phone like that."

"I didn't think so." His eyes were laughing at her, not at all fooled. He held the door open for her. "She must take after me."

"That's it. Every time she misbehaves, that's what I say. She must get that from you, because it isn't me."

"That's not what your family says. They say she is just like you."

That had them both laughing and they stepped outside. She pulled her sunglasses from her purse. "Since I can't deny that, I'm not going to say anything. It's safest."

"I just happen to like you, so I think Madison is perfect. Like her mother." He stopped to open the van's passenger door, stealing a little more of her heart.

"I happen to think you are pretty fine, too, handsome."

"Good, because I'm taking your keys."

And, to her surprise, he plucked them right out of her hand. "Hey, give those back."

"No way. This is a date, this is my vehicle, too, and I'm driving."

"You can't drive yet, can you?"

"Sure. And it's easier this way, since I know where we're going and you don't."

"I'm not going to surrender my beloved minivan just like that. You can give me directions."

"No. I always used to drive, and I'm up to it. So, get in." He smiled, more handsome than ever for his steely stubbornness.

She knew he'd been working so hard in his appointments. The physical therapist had said so over and over.

And she knew why he pushed himself beyond pain and endurance. She laid her hand on his arm, desperately needing to touch him, to draw his strength into her like air. Sunshine fluttered through the trees lining the parking lot, impossible to hold, but visible all the same. Like grace. Like faith. Like hope renewed.

She climbed into the seat, loving that he took hold of her arm to help her, although she didn't need it. It was him she needed. How good it was to see him standing there, stronger, straighter.

He closed the door, walking around the front of the minivan, washed in dappled light, his shoulders once again a broad dependable line. God had not forgotten them, no. She'd known from the moment she'd first received his supervisor's call that God was holding them all in the palm of His hand.

Jonas slid in behind the wheel, seeming eager to drive again. "Don't worry. I remember driving. I remember the day I got my license. My dad took me."

"You told me he was more nervous than you were."

"He was afraid I was going to pass and he and Mom would be nervous wrecks every second I was out driving." There was no mistaking the dip of affection in his voice for the parents who had loved their only child so dearly. He had lost them three weeks after he'd graduated from high school to a head-on Fourth of July car accident, and he had been minorly injured, buckled safely in the backseat. "Their deaths were the reason I wanted to be a trooper."

She nodded, already knowing that, too. "You wanted to repay the kindness the troopers had shown you that evening coming home from watching the fireworks. You wanted to help others, the way you had been helped."

He nodded put on his seat belt and turned the ignition. "Trust me, I wouldn't be driving if I wasn't able."

"I trust you, Jonas." She had never trusted anyone more. She watched while he checked the mirrors and the lot behind them before smoothly accelerating along the street. He was afraid, too, she realized. He might not admit it and he wasn't about to show it, but she knew. These secrets they kept from one another, her fears and his. "You'll be able to work again. I know it."

"Not on patrol. I intend to walk without a cane, but I'll never be strong enough to pass the physical requirements." He put the car in gear and they rolled through the lot toward the street. "I don't like it, but I can accept that."

"You aren't upset?"

"No. When I look at you and the kids, it seems so little to lose. I'm just grateful to be here, Dani."

She smiled. Dani. What he always used to call her. "You've been talking to someone. Doing research on our past."

"Guilty." He grinned as he checked for traffic and made a right-hand turn. "Your brother was most helpful."

"You talked to Spence?"

"Why? You look surprised. Did he and I not get along or something?"

"You two were great buddies. On the volunteer board for the city churches. Doing charity stuff. Playing golf together."

"I play golf?" He chuckled at that.

"I hope so, as there's a brand-new set of quality clubs in the basement storage." A Christmas gift from her.

"Nice. What other hobbies do I have?"

His eyes were twinkling. This was amusing him. Fine, she could have fun with his amnesia, too. "You love classical music."

"I do?"

"Sure. And theater. You love theater, especially Shakespeare."

"You mean the dudes in tights?" His nose crinkled with dismay. "That doesn't seem very manly."

It was nearly impossible to keep a straight face. "The city symphony has a summer series I could get tickets for. Oh, and I think the college is putting on *King Lear*. There was a notice posted at the bookstore, the last time I was in. We could do both. What do you think?"

"No, that doesn't sound right." He laughed. "Are you trying to deceive me?"

"Never. I just couldn't resist. The look on your face is priceless." It felt wonderful to laugh together, to feel the rumble of his happiness roll through her like a spring breeze.

He stopped for a red light and turned to her. "Something tells me we did this a lot."

"We laughed nearly all the time."

"I can see that about us."

"Even when we disagreed, we would wind up laughing. Not all the time, mind you, but mostly. You would say something funny and it would be impossible for me to be mad at you any longer."

"I can't imagine you getting mad."

"Believe me, I did. You are a very maddening man at times, Jonas Lowell. And I'm your wife. I ought to know." She said the words with love, because she'd stopped caring about his stubbornness and his unfailing ability to put off her "to do" list the moment she'd seen him hovering near death in the ICU. "I love you for those things."

"Love does not demand its own way. It keeps no record of when it has been wronged. Love never gives up, never loses faith, is always hopeful, and endures through every circumstance…"

She heard what he did not say; what only could be felt with the heart. Tears filled her eyes and she turned away so he couldn't see them.

The blinker ticked, and he swung the minivan into a fast-food place's drive-through lane.

"Chicken?" he asked while she laughed with delight.

He was reenacting their second date.

"There was a lot that Spence couldn't tell me," Jonas explained as he packed the leftover bucket of chicken and offered her the contents of a small bakery box from Ava's bakery. "Your sister swung by when you were in the shower with more information and these. She says they are your favorite."

"Are they ever. Fudge peanut butter brownies. These weren't on the second date menu, but this is a good improvement."

He was sure glad she thought so. He took one for himself and recovered the box. He set it down so he could sidle a little closer to his wife on the blanket he'd put down in the grass for their picnic. "She said this was a monumental date for us."

"Spence wouldn't know the details, so I wasn't sure if you knew." She blushed prettily, looking at the gurgle of the swiftly moving river in front of them. "You are a good investigator. I wouldn't have thought you would have gone to so much trouble."

"It's for you, Dani. Why wouldn't I?" He ached to brush the worry from her face and all the fears she hadn't told him about. He could see how it was, how well she'd held things together while he'd been fighting that coma. How she had kept the kids' world as normal as possible while he'd been far away in rehabilitation. How she had faithfully supported him with all of her heart when he returned to her, unable to remember a single thing about the life they had built together. "I wanted you to know that I'm in this all the way. I'm not going to leave you alone shouldering everything. That's why I'm working so hard to get back."

"I know. For me and the kids."

The kids. They were sure something, too. God had richly blessed him. Jonas might not remember much, but he knew what a rare gift he had. He eyed the bag Danielle had put into the van that morning, the one she had brought with her now. "You brought the pictures?"

"Every one."

"I thought we might want to look at them instead of going kayaking. I'm not up to that yet." But there were things he could do; he could listen to his wife.

"I was never as outdoorsy as you, so I don't mind that we're skipping the water sports." She finished her brownie and, after licking her fingers, reached for the bag with the pictures in it.

Every little thing she did captivated him. He wondered if after being married for so long, he had stopped noticing the way she bit her bottom lip when she was thinking, or watched him through her lashes to see what he was up to. Had he taken her for granted? These were things he could not ask her.

Her movements were like poetry as she pulled the book from the bag, each movement graceful and deliberate. The sweet scent of the wild grasses, the whisper of the overhead leaves, the music of the river and the blue sky framing her were things he might forget, but not her. He memorized the slope of her cute nose, her wide-set eyes with long lashes, the cut of her cheekbones and her generous mouth, so ready to smile and offer a kind word.

Hers was the first face he'd seen when he'd opened his eyes. Even when he hadn't been able to recognize his own wife, he'd been rendered speechless by the sight of her. She'd made his heart start beating again.

Now, watching her in the simple act of opening the photo album and brushing her fingertips across the plastic-covered pages, he was fascinated by her. By the small smile on her lips, by the glitter of secret happiness in her eyes, by her posture so fluid and straight and her kind goodness that he could not get enough of.

"Here's the first picture I took when we were driving away from Gran's house." She stretched out on the blanket and laid the white album in front of her. "See? There's the family waving to us. You'd left the window open since you had been hanging out of it as we drove away."

"Me? Hanging out of a window? That doesn't seem too dignified."

"Welcome to your life, Jonas. I hate to break it to you, but you are far from dignified."

He stretched out beside her. "That's a hard blow. Here

I was hoping to find out I was this really cool, sophisticated guy."

"Sorry to disappointment you, but had you been, I doubt I would have been interested enough to marry you."

He saw himself, young and whole and fit, suntanned and looking like the happiest man in the world in that limo. "Then I'm glad I'm just an unsophisticated, undignified guy."

She shook her head, amusement making her eyes a deep cinnamon. "I liked you that way. Right after I snapped this picture you put your arm around me and gave me a big kiss."

"That sounds like me." He grinned and leaned closer as she turned the page.

There were more pictures of them arriving at the Bozeman airport and waiting at the gate. It was late; the airport had that overly bright look to the lights against black windows. She must have had a timer and squeezed in beside him at the last second. He looked at the image of his younger self, so tall and straight, with both arms around his bride and how he gazed at his new bride with complete adoration and one hundred percent pure love.

"This is in the Seattle hotel's lobby." She tapped the ribbon-framed image. He was still grinning, as if he considered himself the luckiest man in the world. "We had this beautiful room. We were so exhausted that after you ordered room service for us, since neither of us had hardly eaten all day even with tons of food at the reception and at Gran's house, we fell asleep."

He leaned closer to study the well-appointed suite. He hardly noticed the rich colors and textures of the room because Danielle was in the picture. He must have taken it of her. She looked so bubbly and carefree in a pretty cotton summer dress and sandals. Her hair was a soft fall of curls around her face, different from the Danielle he knew now.

It didn't take a genius to know why. For her face, as she studied these images and remembered the better times of their marriage, had changed, looked less like a woman who was worried, strained and fighting to hide her fears. He could see the woman from the pictures, alight with hope, made even more beautiful with love.

"Here's where we were waiting for our shuttle to the airport. At five-thirty in the morning. See how grumpy I look." The breeze from the river ruffled through her hair and she pushed a lock of curls behind her ear, an innocent gesture.

"You don't look grumpy." Not at all. "You look pretty amazing for five-thirty in the morning."

"I'm glad you still think so. I don't think I photograph well at all. Unlike you. There you are, grinning at me."

He saw more than the picture showed. He saw a young strapping man holding out his hand to his beloved wife. The tenderness in his eyes had changed. Deepened with their love.

He quietly studied the snapshots of their private cottage on the beach in Maui. Somehow she was even more beautiful than ever, translucent with life and love.

He had been the man who had loved her like that, and it was impossible to remember. Impossible to feel now. He groped in his mind and searched deeper in his brain but there was nothing. No hint of a memory. No trace of an image. No whisper of what was past.

"This is when we first went snorkeling." Danielle tapped a plastic-covered image of him smiling at her, feet flippers on, waving one of them at her. "You'd been before, but I hadn't. I was not too sure I wanted to go into the water where all those fish and slimy things were. Oh, and sharks."

"I already knew how to snorkel?"

"And to scuba dive, which we did—" she turned several colorful pages "—here."

Page after page, in one picture after another, he learned more than the sequence of events that had happened on their honeymoon trip. He saw how with every day there were tiny changes between them. The way they looked at one another. The happiness they radiated. The quiet unspoken tie that bound them together increased in strength and was as unmistakable as the spectacular Maui shore.

Love had done this, changing them, improving them, polishing them day by day. Love that he was going to find again, Jonas vowed, reaching out to brush a stray curl behind his wife's ear.

Chapter Nine

They couldn't have had a nicer time, Danielle thought, relaxing in the passenger seat. How nice to have her husband driving again. He was right, he was doing just fine. For a while they drove in companionable silence. She could almost pretend everything hadn't changed between them. That the bullet had never struck Jonas. That their family and their marriage were whole.

"I turn here?" he asked, picking up the city streets well. He'd always had an excellent sense of direction.

"Yes."

The complex had been shining new in the fifties, and had a dated look, but that was about to change. She watched Jonas navigate around orange cones in the parking lot and they waved to her brother-in-law Brice, whose company was starting the renovation. She spotted Spence through the long row of front windows in the bookstore. As usual, he appeared dark and glowering. Poor Spence.

Jonas turned off the engine. "It's good to be back in the saddle again."

"It *is* good," she agreed. "We'll have to get your truck back from Spence. It's not good for a vehicle to sit without being driven, so he took it not long after you were injured. He's been maintaining it for you."

"Yep, I'm going to need that back," Jonas agreed. "You've been doing too much, Dani. Running me from appointment to appointment. Keeping up with the kids. I can run myself now, and help out with the other stuff."

"I'm not going to argue with that, handsome. I can use the help." That was an understatement if there ever was one, she thought as she gathered up the bundle of papers from the backseat and led the way into the bookstore.

As expected, Spence's frown hardened into a grimace. "I'm dreading looking at the profit-and-loss statement. I've got a bank meeting in the morning and I don't want bad news."

She wished Spence wouldn't worry so much. She wished a lot of things when it came to her big brother. He had been an incredible support over the past year, always there when she needed him, always pitching in without her having to ask. But he was unhappy in his personal life and growing colder with each passing year. She loved him and so she tried not to let his scowl bother her. "It's not bad at all."

"Thank heavens."

He took his responsibilities toward their family seriously, she knew, shouldering all of their worries. She handed him the binders. "Here. I have two copies. One for the loan person, and one for you."

"Thanks, Dani." His scowl faded. "This is a big relief. I know you're busy, but with the complex's construction loans—"

"I know." She squeezed his hand, wishing she could help him the way he helped her. "Let me know if you need anything else, okay? Where's Katherine? I thought she had her reading group today."

"She does. Everyone is here, but I couldn't call them in time to cancel." There was his scowl, returning full force. "She said she wasn't feeling well, so I made her go home. I put in a call to Jack, too, but I got his voice mail."

"She's probably just tired." At least, she hoped that's all it was. She fished the phone out of her purse pocket. "I'll check on her. Does Mom know this?"

Spence shook his head, scattering his short brown hair. "She took Madison to her lesson, right?"

"And out to lunch and ice cream, but I suspect not in that order. She was going to pick up Tyler from church, too, and make a day of it with them."

"I didn't want to disrupt that. I saw Jonas is back behind the wheel." Spence nodded toward the front of the store.

Danielle glanced up after hitting the speed dial. Jonas had been stopped at the front of the store by a member of their church and a patron of the bookstore, Lucy Chapin. They were talking, and as their voices carried, she could tell that Lucy was explaining how she and Jonas knew one another.

While Katherine's phone began to ring, Danielle watched her brother carefully. He seemed to be eyeing the front of the store very intently, and it wasn't Jonas he watched. Could it be that their loner of a brother hid a secret interest in pretty and funny Lucy?

"H-hello?" said a strained, tired-sounding voice on the other end of the connection.

"Katherine?" Danielle hardly recognized her own sister's voice. "Kath, are you all right?"

"I don't want you to worry. I'm resting, and I'm waiting for the doctor to call me b-back." There was the faintest hint of fear in her seemingly calm voice.

Katherine was like that, so strong even in crisis. Danielle's pulse kicked with worry. "I'm coming over. I'll be there in a few minutes."

"No, you don't have to. You have enough on your plate with Jonas. I have this under control. I have my feet up and I'm staying quiet until—" There was a bump in the line. "Oh, can you hold on, Dani? That's the doctor."

"Sure." Danielle heard a click and waited, praying that everything was going to be fine. Katherine had wanted a baby for a long time now. She deserved to have this pregnancy go smoothly. She deserved to be a mom.

Worry hooked her and automatically she turned to Jonas, her gaze fastening on his across the top of the new-arrivals display. Unlike old times, Jonas didn't instantly know what she meant without words. He no longer understood her more than she did herself. But he did head toward her, moving swiftly with his cane. Before she knew it, his free hand enfolded hers and he towered above her, all concern.

Spence rubbed the back of his neck. "What's wrong? What did she say?"

"I'm on hold while she talks with the doctor."

"The doctor?"

She was glad for Jonas's hand, comforting in hers.

The phone clicked, and Katherine spoke. "Dani? I need to get to the hospital, but I'm not supposed to drive. I can't reach Jack."

"One of us will be there in a few minutes. You hang tight, okay?" She kept her voice calm; it sure made a difference having Jonas with her. Clear and calm through the worry, she glanced at Spence, who nodded once and took off for the parking lot, pulling his keys out of his trouser pocket as he ran. "Katherine? Spence is on his way. He'll be there in less than two minutes. You just stay calm."

"I'm trying to." Katherine did sound steadier than she had. "I'm trusting the Lord with this, that the baby will be okay."

"I trust Him, too." Danielle knew firsthand that things didn't always turn out right, even if you did everything possible. She prayed that this would not be one of those times. "Are you in any pain?"

"I have a terrible headache. I would feel better if I could reach Jack, but I think he's in some sort of a meeting."

Jonas chose that moment to pull away from her, giving her a reassuring look as he made his way to the front desk. He spoke to the cashier, and she handed him the phone receiver.

Who was he calling? Danielle wondered, and then she knew. He was calling his old office. The number was probably still on the list of emergency numbers Spence always kept taped to the counter.

"Don't worry," she told her sister. "Jonas will find Jack for you."

"Bless him. He's one of the good guys."

"I know." Danielle's voice faltered. So much had changed. So much had gone wrong. And yet none of it, not even the unfairness of that single bullet nor the painful fight through his physical rehabilitation had changed the good in Jonas.

"Wait, that's him calling in." Katherine sounded relieved. "Thank Jonas for me."

With a click, the connection ended. Danielle closed her phone and dropped it into her purse, hardly aware of anything except the man watching her from the counter. His gaze was steady, his stance solid, and his heart right there for her to see.

"Thank you." Her voice failed, so she had to mouth the words, but she knew he heard them just the same.

"My pleasure." He came her way, always her hero. "You might want to call your mom."

"Right." Her brain wasn't working, but she fished her phone back out of her purse anyway. Jonas had always been able to do that to her, even after seven, no, nearly eight years of marriage—their anniversary was coming up soon. "Spence must be at her door by now. I'll have Mom meet them. Oh, wait. I have to get the kids from her."

"Tell you what. Why don't I take 'em, and you and your mom can go together to check on your sister." Composed, problem-solving, that was Jonas.

"I should stay with you." She sorted through the numbers on the phone's electronic list. "I can visit Katherine later."

"How many times did Katherine come to the hospital for your sake, when I was there?" His voice came rough with emotion. "How much did she do for you while I was in the hospital or away at the rehab clinic?"

"More than I could begin to count." Her family had been her foundation when Jonas had been unconscious. Their love had held her up when she hadn't been sure she could go on. All the thousand things they did without once being asked.

"Then you should go." His hand found her shoulder and

settled there. His touch reminded her of all the times he had been her comfort, her support, her foundation. "Come on, we'll meet your mom, and I'll take the kids home."

More respect for this man glowed to life deep within her. For a moment—just one moment—she allowed herself to lean against his chest and savor the familiar beat of his heart.

"Daddy!" Madison jumped up from dressing her doll, and the kitchen lights reflected on her jeweled tiara. "I getta answer the phone! I getta!"

Jonas closed the freezer door, set the frozen box on the counter and lifted the cordless receiver from the cradle. Madison bounced up and down at his knee, her doll with her. His daughter's little hands were already reaching up, the doll tucked in her elbow. Her fingers grasped the receiver, but he got a glance at the caller ID. He hit the button for her, but she was already talking.

"Hello! Hello! How are yew?"

He could hear Danielle's gentle laughter and then her soft alto saying, "Hello, bubbles," before Madison tucked the phone snugly against her ear, button-cute, and began chattering away to her mommy.

Emotion balled up in his throat. It was starting to sink in exactly what he'd lost. What that speeder with an outstanding warrant and a gun had taken away from him. Battling down darker emotions, he ripped open the end of the box and slid the frozen pizza onto the big cookie sheet.

In the other room, the door slid shut and footsteps pounded through the living room. Tyler burst into sight, breathless and sprinkled with water droplets. "Dad! Dad! I put out a four-alarm blaze. Me and my men had a tough time."

The little boy looked up at him with excitement shining on his face and love in his eyes. Tyler's warm wet hand grabbed his and held on so tight. "We coulda used some help, though. Dad, can you come, too? After supper? Can ya?"

"Sure, son." Jonas's chest fluttered with unstoppable affection. The hand in his felt so small, so fragile, and held on with such need. How many imaginary fires had Tyler been forced to put out alone, because his dad wasn't here to help him? Unquenchable anger surged through him, but it wasn't nearly as strong as his love for his boy. "I'll report to duty for the evening shift, Captain."

"Okay!" Tyler's grin was instant and impossibly wide. He broke away and yanked open the refrigerator. "Me and my men could use a break. We're gonna get some rest and some fuel and then hit the line again."

Right there in the middle of the kitchen with the oven beeper signaling that the oven was up to heat, and with Madison telling her mommy all about the new fancy sandals from Grammy, Jonas felt the distance the last year had put between him and his children. He'd studied the photo albums. Evidence of what he lost was right in front of him and plastered in wooden frames on the walls surrounding him.

He'd lost the last year of helping Tyler play fireman in the backyard and of watching Madison grow from a gurgling toddler to a talking little girl. He'd lost snuggles and laughter and time with each of them, precious time that was lost forever. Time that was ticking away even now as he poured his son a cup of juice.

He felt like the stranger, the outsider, fighting so hard to get back what he'd lost; he was only now seeing how impossible that job was. He loved his kids—there was no doubt about that. Whether he remembered them or not, no matter what the future brought. But it was time to get to know them, time to stop trying to gather memories that were already gone—and time to enjoy them right now.

Unbearable anger spiked through him like the sharp edge of a fireman's axe, anger at the man who'd done this to his family. To his children. As he slid the pizza into the oven, he realized how much he hated all the moments of all the days that he hadn't been here to ruffle Tyler's brown hair, as he was doing now. Or to swing Madison up into his arms and to feel her fine baby hair against his jaw. He wanted to crush the man who had stolen so much from his children. From him.

He blew out a breath, realizing he was shaking with unfamiliar feelings, which he did not know how to deal with. As he watched Tyler chug down a glass of juice, the emotion kept building. He felt helpless beneath the power of it, helpless to know what to do.

"Daddy! It's for yew!" Madison held out the phone.

"Thank you, princess." He gave her a smacking kiss to her cheek, took the phone and set her carefully on her feet. She ran away, screeching after her brother, who was headed for the cookie jar, taking her doll with her.

"Jonas, I'm on my way home. Katherine is fine, but they're keeping her overnight for observation."

Danielle's voice filled his ear, his thoughts, his heart. He had to clear the emotion from his throat before he could speak. "Th-that's great. It was nothing serious?"

"Her blood pressure was way too high, but she's on medication that should take care of that. What do you want me to pick up for dinner?"

He checked the time. "Don't bother. Just come straight home. I miss you."

"I miss you, too, handsome. I'm just a few minutes away." After she said goodbye, she disconnected.

Jonas sighed, a little lonely without her.

"Dad! Can we have one?" Tyler's hand was halfway to the counter as he gave a beseeching look.

Cute kid. Jonas's heart gave a thump. "I'd let you, but your mom is on her way and something tells me, she won't."

"Pleeeaase?" Madison, standing next to her brother, pleaded with steepled hands.

This was his first stab at saying no. At being a real parent. He drew himself up, ready for the job. "Not now. Why don't you two go wait for—" And there was the sound of the garage door opening.

"It's Mommy!" Madison dashed through the kitchen, each sandal step striking sharp against the linoleum as she raced to meet her mother. Tyler followed her, dripping sprinkler water as he went. Their calls to their mom and their chatter when she opened the door rang like happy music through the house.

His dark emotions and anger had no place here. Jonas stuffed them down and grabbed four plastic cups from the cupboard and limped his way across the kitchen, leaving his cane behind. Those emotions were holding him back, and he had a family to stand tall for. A wife to win back. Somehow his anger rose to the surface, anger he had to defeat. He would not let it touch what was precious in his life.

He set the cups on the edge of the table in the dining room adorned with family photos, and his gaze felt drawn to the framed, professional-sized picture with a wooden frame and elaborate matting. It was no ordinary picture, and not one of their family. Radiating beauty, it was a collector's piece with a numbered tag tucked into the frame.

The simple shot was of a snow-covered evergreen branch. A mantle of pristine snow draped an evergreen's uplifted bough. The limb reached upward like an arm to a stormy, roiling sky. A storm was breaking, gold and peach rays of the sun broke like hope through dismal clouds. *Hebrews 11:1* was written in the corner, beneath a familiar signature.

Jonas remembered the text, and the words tugged at his heart like a comfort and a censure. *Now faith is being sure of what we hope for and certain of what we do not see.*

Yes, he thought, anger had no place in his heart, but faith did.

"See, Mommy, see?" Madison skipped into the room, her tiara askew. "I got a pink *and* a purple pair."

"I see. Your grammy is spoiling you. Ice cream and new shoes?" Over the top of their daughter's head, Danielle smiled at him. "What's all this? There's a bowl of fresh salad on the counter. Sliced garlic bread. And the table's set."

"Oh. I made dinner." He went back to work setting the cups around the table. "It's only frozen pizza, but it'll be piping hot and on the table in fifteen minutes."

"*Only* frozen pizza? Jonas, I can't believe you did this. You've done everything."

"Well, I haven't solved world hunger or anything, but if it makes things easier for you, then I'm happy."

"You have." Danielle took in the neatly set table, including paper napkins folded beneath the flatware, and the kitchen so tidy and clean. Jonas had done more than simply start dinner. He'd straightened up. He'd cleaned up the breakfast dishes she'd left in the sink. The day's mail, including the bills, was neatly stacked next to the phone. He'd taken care of the kids, who were bubbling with happiness after spending a few hours with their daddy.

Their wonderful daddy. She ached with tenderness for this man. He was trying too hard, she could see the strain paling his face, but did it show in his voice or manner? No. There was only his endearing, lopsided grin and kindness.

She kissed Madison's cheek, leaving her to her doll. Jonas had no idea, she was sure, of all the evenings she'd been alone with the kids, even before he'd been hurt. He had no idea the busyness of their lives had been putting distance between them, little spaces at a time.

"Pizza's ready." Jonas's announcement was met with cheers from the little ones. "Tyler, will you get the oven gloves for me?"

The boy raced to obey, running to the stack of drawers next to the stove and hauling out the matching pink gingham mitts. He held them out, proud to be helping his father. Jonas took the gloves, fitting them onto his hands— somehow the pink mitts only emphasized his manliness— and opened the oven.

Tyler tipped his head back, gazing up at Jonas with wonder and awe on his face, as if the bullet had never happened. Air caught in her lungs. What mattered had not changed.

Her husband took out three trays from the oven. Two held pizzas, and the other held Tater Tots.

Not exactly the healthiest meal, but definitely comfort food. Food she was absolutely in need of now. Tyler was elated to be assisting his dad by digging through the drawer for a spatula and watching while Jonas scooted the steaming greasy tots onto a big platter.

"Goody! I love taters!" Madison clapped her hands together with surprised glee, and took off for the fridge. "I gotta have lotza catch-up!"

"Hold on there, bubbles." Danielle caught the door and before Madison could empty out the refrigerator in search of the ketchup bottle, she pointed it out to her. "Right there, troubles."

"I take it to the table for Daddy!" Madison clutched the plastic bottle with both hands, extracted it from the shelf in the door, knocking over a bottle of pickles, and took off in a flat-footed run to the table.

Danielle righted the bottle and closed the door. "What a good girl."

"I know." Madison pushed the bottle onto the edge of the table with both hands.

She set her purse next to the phone and noticed the bills. Best not to think about those right now. She reached for Madison's hand. "Time to wash up. Come on, princess."

"No-ooooo!" Madison shrieked, jerking back. "I kin do it!"

The doorbell rang, saving them all from Madison's temper. As Tyler hurried to the door, Danielle glanced out the window over the sink. Spence's big green truck was parked in the driveway.

"Uncle Spence!" Tyler called out as the door swung open.

"Sorry, I should have called, Dani." Spence strode in, bringing the shadows with him. "Jonas said I could just come by. I'm on my way over to check on Katherine's house for her. She's got some roses I'm supposed to water."

"Uncle Spence!" Madison flew toward him, arms outstretched. She giggled when he swept her up into the air.

"You get prettier every time I see you. How come you're so pretty?"

"I'm a princess." Madison snuggled against him. "Wanna see my doll?"

"Come see the fire I put out!" Tyler grabbed his uncle by the hand.

That was Spence, tough on the outside and good with fragile flowers and small children. She'd always had an enormous soft spot for her big brother. "Do you want to stay and eat with us? I think the kids would sure love it."

"Oh, I don't want to put you out."

Jonas spoke up. "Not at all. We'd love to have you. Stay and enjoy my—" He paused, as if searching for the word. "Cooking masterpiece?"

"Culinary." Danielle helped him out and, so that Spence wasn't overwhelmed, took Madison into her arms. "That is, if you consider pizza and Tater Tots high cuisine."

"It is in my book." Spence still looked worried and strained, but he managed a short, brief half grin. "Jonas, did someone drop by the extra set of store keys?"

"Yep." Jonas nodded toward the entry hall on his way to the table, pizza sheets in hand. "Lucy, the one I met at the store? She came by with them."

"*She* closed up for me?" Spence winced. "They couldn't get anyone else?"

That was a pretty convincing act, Danielle thought. If she hadn't noticed his quick glance in the pretty blonde's direction today, she would have believed him now. She understood why he tried so hard to deny the truth, perhaps even to himself. "Isn't tonight singles Bible study over at the church? I'm guessing your staff didn't want to be late for it. It sounds pretty generous of Lucy to have offered to stay and lock up the bookstore."

Spence passed a hand over his face. "No, I know. I'll need to thank her. Maybe I'll send a note."

"A phone call would be better." Danielle couldn't resist a tiny suggestion. "Or, you might want to repay her for her trouble. Maybe a nice dinner?"

"I know what you're up to. You're no better than Katherine, trying to match me up with that woman." Spence scowled, but his eyes looked so sad as he headed toward the fridge. "You kids want juice?"

"Yay!"

"Yip!"

Spence, as always, made himself useful by carrying the juice bottle to the table and began pouring for the kids. She caught Jonas watching her. There was that gentleness again, making his eyes deepen. Jonas no longer reached out to pull her snugly against his chest, rest his chin on the top of her head and enfold her in his strong arms. She wished he would. She needed him so much, but she tried to be patient and she tried to trust where God was leading them.

If only it were easier. The loneliness within her—the kind that only Jonas could drive away—settled like a weight in her soul.

"I get to say grace?" Tyler pleaded, as he climbed into his chair. "Pleeaase?"

"Mommy!" Madison grabbed Danielle by the hand and tugged.

The children needed her. No, needed *them*. So she gathered her determination and let her daughter lead her to the table, where her husband, bless him, held her chair out for her. Something he hadn't done in years.

Chapter Ten

After a quick stop at the florist the next morning, Danielle headed straight to the hospital, the same one where Jonas had stayed for so long. She'd gone there so many times the minivan could probably drive itself. She pulled into visitor parking, grabbed her purse and the bouquet of cheerful flowers and headed toward the entrance in the fresh summer sunshine.

As she walked the somber halls, it was the little things that flashed her back to that horrible afternoon, almost a year ago now. The tap, tap of her shoes and the strange echo of noises against the bleak long walls. The antiseptic and sadness in the air made her mouth go dry and fear taste coppery on her tongue. She'd walked down a corridor just like this one on her way to see Jonas in ICU for the first time. She'd prayed so hard then, and she prayed as hard now for her sister's sake.

"Dani! Over here." Ava poked out of a doorway and waved, her wedding ring sparkling in the light. She looked as adorable as ever with her blond hair and big sparkling eyes. "They're sending Katherine home today. Good news, huh? But wait, how are things on your end? I hear that Jonas took you on a second date and *drove*."

"He did. He's doing very well."

"He'll be as good as new soon, you just wait." Ava grabbed her hand and gave her a heartening squeeze.

Danielle prayed that Ava was right. She had so many worries and it was harder to withstand them without her best friend, her husband. "I should probably take these to her house, then. I imagine—"

Welcomes interrupted her. "Dani!" "Hi, stranger." "Good morning, baby," all rose simultaneously from the cluster of her family around Katherine's bed.

"—that Kath has about a zillion flowers," she finished, noticing the colorful arrangements on every available surface of the room. "Good morning. I should have known it was standing room only."

Mom broke free, arms wide, to give her a hug. "You look tired. What can I do for you? How about I swing by and help you out with the housework after we get Katherine settled?"

"No, Mom. I should be helping you."

"Dani, thanks for the flowers." Katherine looked tired and pale, but other than that, good. Jack was at her side, a big strapping man, holding her hand as if he never intended to let go.

"You have a rose garden here already. I don't think there's any room for my contribution. Katherine, you look perky." Dani stopped at the foot of the bed, taking in the sight of her older sister. Her stepsister, sure, but love had made them real sisters.

"I am perky compared to yesterday." Katherine managed a real smile.

"You'll feel even better when you're back in your own bed. I'm guessing they're putting you on bed rest?"

"You guessed right." Katherine rolled her eyes heavenward. "I'll do anything for the baby, absolutely. But I'm hoping that heaven is going to be kind when I have to tell Spence that Ava and Aubrey have abandoned him, and I'm the only family left that's working for him."

Jack added a little forcefully, "I'm telling him, and I'll make sure he's nice about it. He wants the best for you."

"Speaking of him, where is he?" Danielle glanced around the room, nodding to her dad, and her other sisters. "He must have opened the bookstore?"

"No one's heard from him." Katherine shrugged. "I suspect he's upset about this. You know how he gets. Whenever he feels any emotion whatsoever he works even harder."

Mom shuffled vases at the windowsill. "Heaven knows I've tried with that boy. John, what are you going to do about our son?"

"Ignore it and hope things right themselves on their own?" Dad quipped.

Dorrie chuckled. "How did I know? Girls, witness your father's philosophy on everything these days. Look what I have to contend with."

"Totally terrible." Ava gave Dad a squeeze in fun. "As for Spence, no sane woman is going to have him if he keeps this up, and guess what that means? Yep, that we'll never get rid of him. You have to help him, Dad. The rest of us have tried and failed."

"You don't think I've tried?" Dad sighed, and although they were talking about Spence with love, there was no mistaking the sadness on their father's face. "I've tried more than you know."

Danielle couldn't hold it in any longer. "Guess who locked up the store for Spence yesterday after he ran out to take care of you, Kath?"

Katherine sat up a little straighter. "You mean he just left, without putting anyone in charge?"

"All he cared about was getting to you because Jack couldn't. And yes, Lucy locked up."

"Lucy Chapin?" Ava's jaw dropped. "I thought he couldn't stand her."

"All I know is that she dropped the keys by our house and left them with Jonas, since our house isn't far from Spence's." Hope, that's what she saw on her family's faces. "She volunteered to do it, which means—"

"She wanted to help Spence!" Ava burst out. "This is totally super-duper. Katherine, you called it. You said you thought Spence might be interested in her."

Dad looked around, a little confused, and Mom, after so many years of marriage, knew his question and asked it for him. "Who's this Lucy? Is she a nice girl?"

"The nicest," Lauren said reassuringly, who pitched in whenever the staffing situation was dire at the bookstore. "She belongs to a couple of reader groups, and comes by to sign whenever she has a new book out. You couldn't meet anyone nicer."

"A book? You mean she's an author? Oh, so she's a career woman." Dad seemed to say that as though it wasn't a good thing.

And it probably wasn't, not for Spence. Still, there was hope. Danielle knew it.

Her phone rang, its electronic tune muffled by her purse. Her home number was on the screen. "Excuse me," she said over her shoulder, heading toward the hall.

"Dani?" Jonas's baritone sounded so good. "Spence just showed up. I wanted to check with you. He needs some help setting things up at Katherine's house. I told him I'd like to pitch in. Katherine's stepdaughter has offered to watch the kids. I wanted to check in with you and make sure it was okay."

Unexpected tears scorched the backs of her eyelids. To think that here he was, ready to run off and help out the family with Spence, tied her up in inexplicable knots. He was getting stronger by the day, his speech was improving, and the memory he did have was very good. God had been more than gracious by answering her prayers and bringing Jonas back to them.

It was enough. She had to stop wishing for what she didn't have. Especially when she was deeply grateful for what she did have.

"Of course, that's a great idea." She hoped her voice sounded normal and not strained with emotion. "I'll meet you at Jack and Katherine's house."

"Good. I'll look forward to seeing you."

Her heart filled at the sincerity in his words. She could picture him in her mind's eye, standing so stalwart, a stronger man for all the hardship he had been through and conquered. She couldn't wait to see him.

Jonas. The moment she set foot inside Katherine's front door, loaded down with groceries, her gaze roved to where he stood in the living room. He was moving a small end table into place next to a double bed. Dad and Spence were repositioning the television in the corner, and they called out a greeting. But she only had eyes for her husband.

Jonas might be leaning on a cane, but he looked good giving the table a final tug. Very good. It was as if the scent of the hospital still clung to her and the hard memories with it. She forced the image of seeing him in ICU from her thoughts, when he'd been nearly lifeless and unable to breathe on his own. Gladness filled her at how far he had come.

"Hey, beautiful." Jonas's baritone sounded intimate and caring, although they were far from alone. "I told your dad and Spence that we need a woman's opinion before Katherine sees this for the first time. She might not like what Jack wanted done to her living room."

She loved the glimmer of humor in his eyes. She tried not to think of all the long-standing jokes between them. Of the times when he might have said, "The wife is in charge of the house, shouldn't Jack know that?"

But that was the old Jonas. This Jonas was different, but still hers. Yes, she thought, her heart soaring, he was all hers.

She considered the view of the living room, limited by the full paper bags she was clutching. "I'm not sure what Katherine is going to think. The bed doesn't exactly match her couch."

Dad stepped away, studying the angle of the television. "Sure, but she'll be able to spend her days downstairs, instead of cooped up in the bedroom all day for the next five months."

"Sure, it's a good idea," Danielle agreed. It was awfully sweet of Jack. "Katherine will be very comfortable here, but you might want to move the second couch back in here. Somehow. If there's room."

Jonas rubbed his chin, considering. "We could move the bookcase out and put the couch against the wall. Dani's right. The whole family is going to be trooping in and out of here, and what about holidays? You'll need room enough for everyone to sit."

"I hadn't thought that far." Dad's grin was sheepish. "I can see I have some long-term planning to do. Okay, Spence, ready to manhandle that bookcase?"

Spence scowled, but that was normal for him. "Ready when you are, Dad."

Danielle was vaguely aware of Mom bustling on to the kitchen, of Dad and Spence hefting up the bookcase, apparently hoping all the books would stay in place. All she could focus on was Jonas coming toward her. She might not be able to tell what he was thinking, but he looked happy, as if contributing had brought him a sense of purpose.

"Let me take those for you." He scooped his arm around the bags, so close she could see the smooth-shaven texture of his jaw and the midnight flecks in his eyes.

Any nearer and it would be nothing at all for him to lean in for a kiss. Sweet longing filled her, and she forced her gaze down to the grocery bags he took from her arms.

"These are heavy." He winked at her, as if to let her know that they weren't too heavy for him. "What do you have in here?"

"A few boulders. A barbell or two." She loved that her gentle joke made him laugh as he kept at her side, his cane muted by the carpet.

Mom was in the kitchen, already at work with cabinets open and the pantry door flung wide and pots of differing sizes setting on the stove. "Just put them on the counter there, Jonas," she was saying.

Danielle's gaze went to the wide windows and the backyard where teenage Hayden leaped through the sprinkler with Tyler and Madison. Tyler was laughing, Madison was squealing with each blast of the sprinkler, and the high sound penetrated the glass doors quite easily.

If her heart wasn't airborne before, it was now. Her kids were happy and healthy, as was her husband. It was blessing enough.

Jonas's hand settled lightly on her shoulder. "Your pregnancies were okay, weren't they?"

The worry in his voice—the concern for her—brought the burning feeling back to her eyes. "Yes. I was great. I sailed right through all nine months, both times. There were no complications."

"Whew. I'm glad." He didn't move, his hand a steady comfort, and his touch a soothing balm.

For the first time in what felt like ages, she didn't feel sorely alone. All the ways she had needed her husband over the last year ached within her—all but one. She soaked in his comforting touch and felt it strengthen her.

"Uh-oh," he whispered in her ear. "They spotted you."

"Mommeeeee!" Madison raced to the door, stretched up on tiptoe to reach the handle and shove it open. Her bare feet pitter-pattered on the tile floor. Water sluiced off her little pink T-shirt and yellow flowered walking shorts as she came barreling straight at Danielle, arms out. "I runned and I won!"

"You did?" Danielle knelt down, delighting in the soggy hug. She gave her dripping daughter a kiss on the cheek.

"Yip! I'll shew you!" Off she went, feet slapping. "Come see! I can go fast!"

"I'm watching," Danielle called out as the door swept open and the little girl took off through the lush green grass, running straight toward the sprinkler.

Jonas's hand remained a gentle presence on her shoulder. He leaned closer, his jaw brushing against her hair. "Was it always like this?"

"Yes. Things are getting back to normal."

"I can see why we had date nights. I had a tough time getting you alone."

There was a smile in his voice, a smile that made hope leap into her heart. Before she could respond, a loud thunk, thunk, thunk rose from the staircase.

Dad called out, "Jonas. Uh…any chance you can come help out?"

"Be right there." He withdrew his hand and moved away from her.

Danielle watched him walk away, her husband, her world. Her heart was full of love for him. It should be enough, but she couldn't seem to stop hoping that her love would be returned.

Noises from the kitchen behind her reminded her that she was not alone. That the door to the backyard stood open and children's laughter rose sweetly with the breeze.

Mom came close to rifle through one of the grocery bags Jonas had put on the counter for her. "Are you okay, baby?"

Love. She had so much of it. How could she rightfully pine for the one love she didn't have? She turned to her mom, who watched her with concern. "I'm fine. I can make the spaghetti sauce if you want to go check on the men. Something tells me they need a woman's advice."

Another thump, thump came from upstairs.

"You're right. I'd best keep my eye on them. You're sure that you're all right? Being in the hospital today had to make you remember when Jonas was in there. We all remembered, honey."

Danielle's throat felt thick. "That is all behind us. We're here for Katherine now. She's going to get all the tender loving care she can stand."

"Exactly." Mom skirted the corner of the counter. "I'd best get up there before some disaster happens. Oh, look at Madison. She left the door open."

"I'll close it, Mom. Go rescue the men." Danielle went to close the door, and sure enough, Madison screeched to a halt in the wet grass.

"Mommeeeee! Look at me!" She took off in a run, little legs churning and feet flying.

A loud thump sounded directly over her head. She heard a flurry of voices, muffled by the ceiling, and Jonas's calm baritone, rumbling in reassurance.

Her love for Jonas crashed through her like an ocean wave. It swept away her doubts and her fears for the moment, leaving everything in her heart fresh and whole and without limits.

The drive home was not a quiet one. Danielle spent most of her time trying to quiet Madison, who'd missed her afternoon nap and felt it, poor baby. No amount of comfort would soothe away the little girl's upset over being strapped into her car seat. Tyler was revved up, talking a mile a minute over the top of her sobs of rage. Jonas seemed exhausted, although it did not show in his driving, which he insisted on doing, as the man of the house.

Exhaustion hung heavily on her, too. She'd grocery shopped with mom, cooked lunch for the crowd and helped her mom bake three low-sodium casseroles for the rest of the week. They'd chopped fresh veggies and bagged them for snacks. They'd washed the kitchen, did every dish, made the bed in the living room and set up as many conveniences as they could for Katherine.

The only saving grace was in knowing that she was home safe and sound, feeling better, and that her sudden onset of mild preeclampsia was being medicated and monitored.

"She's going to be all right," Jonas reassured her as he pulled onto their street. "Jack's protective. If he didn't think she should have left the hospital, she wouldn't have."

"I believe it." Jack was nearly as impressive as Jonas, but then Danielle had to admit she carried a huge bias. No man was better than her husband. No man. "You did so much for my family today."

"For *our* family." He kept his attention on the road and spoke evenly over Madison's "Noooooo! Hate the buckle!" and Tyler's advice to his sister not to sweat it, you gotta wear a seat belt. "I see how it was when I was hurt. They're there for us. We're there for them. It's what you do for people you love."

His words struck her. *It's what you do for people you love.* He used to say that all the time. It was a phrase she hadn't heard since his injury.

Did that mean he was starting to remember? To come

back to himself? She was too tired to filter her emotions and tears filled her eyes. It took all her strength to blink them away.

An electronic tune rang out, hard to hear with all the noise from the backseat, and she fished her cell phone from her purse. It was a long-distance number she didn't recognize. "Hello?"

"Danielle? It's me." Aubrey's voice sounded worried. "I just talked with Mom, and I'm really unhappy with you all right now. Someone should have told me about Katherine earlier than this. William's rearranging our flights."

"That's why we didn't call you." Danielle loved her sister for her caring heart. "We knew you would be on the next available flight home, and Katherine and the baby are going to be fine."

"She's not fine. They put her in the hospital."

"As a precaution. She had a sudden rise in blood pressure, but she's all right now."

"She's on bed rest. That's not all right. I should be there to help her."

"You should be with your husband on your honeymoon. Kath has the rest of us at her beck and call."

"But will she—" Aubrey paused, as if what she had to say would be too painful. "Will she lose the baby?"

"Not if she takes care of herself. That's what we're all making sure of. It's a minor complication, is all. At least at this point." Danielle understood her sister's worries. She had them, too. "Promise me you'll finish out your stay. Call Katherine if you have to. I'm sure that's what she will want."

"I don't want to trouble her—"

"She'd love to talk with you. If you're lucky, you'll catch Mom and Rebecca. They were still there when we left. I think Rebecca was doing all the laundry, and Mom was scrubbing bathrooms."

"Not that Katherine's house needed that, as it's always spotless, but that's Mom for you." Aubrey sighed, love clear in her voice. "All right. I'll call Katherine and make sure. But if we stay, then I want your word, Dani. You have to call if there's any change. I mean it."

"I promise."

"Good. And I'll call anyway just to check."

Danielle saw Jonas glance at her as he stopped in the driveway, and she hit the garage door remote clipped to the visor in front of her. "You enjoy Fiji, and bring back lots of pictures."

"Okay. Give Jonas and the kids my love."

Danielle said goodbye and hung up to find Jonas still watching her. "Aubrey has a hard time being so far away from us."

"I can understand that." It was too dark to see much of his expression, but his baritone rumbled pleasantly. "She's the twin that got married, right?"

"Right."

"See? I'm getting this. I'll be back to normal soon."

She remembered what he'd said on their first reenacted date, standing on the bridge. *I'm disabled. That's what they call me now and it makes you sad. You need a whole man. A strong husband.*

Her dear, sweet Jonas. "Normal? We were never normal, handsome."

"Are you saying we were abnormal?"

His joke made both of them smile.

"We were blessed. We still are blessed." She dropped

the cell phone back into her purse, looking down into the shadows, hiding her face, hiding the breadth of her love for him.

"I'm not doubting that, Danielle. I can see how God has blessed me. But you—" He took a breath, as if gathering up his courage and the right words. "I'm fighting for you. You're going to get back the man you married."

Her chin came up and she forgot to protect her heart. "Oh, Jonas, trust me. I love you just the way you are." *Even if you do not love me.* She bit back those words, keeping them inside, already hearing the silence settle between them.

Without a word, Jonas eased the minivan into the garage, and the moment between them had been shattered. She'd spoken her feelings too soon, shocking him, probably making him feel pressure to feel what he did not.

He shut off the engine, and to the sound of Tyler tumbling out of his car seat and Madison's sniffles, he turned to her. "I don't remember how much I loved you, Dani, but I want to."

He pressed a kiss to her cheek, chaste and promising, her answered prayer.

Chapter Eleven

Danielle faced another day, as she always did, both remembering those quiet mornings before the kids were born when she'd had time for prayer, devotional reading and reflection over her morning cup of coffee—and being grateful for the constant noise, motion and refereeing.

"Madison, don't you climb up on the dresser." Danielle blew the shank of hair out of her eyes and opened the closet door. "You are troubles, bubbles."

"But I'm a hummingbird, Mommy. Hayden said I was fast just like one." She stuck out her arms and hummed.

And didn't move a muscle from the opened dresser drawer, second from the bottom, where she had one foot in, one foot out. How long that was going to hold, was anyone's guess.

"Hummingbirds don't climb on dressers." Danielle knowing full well what her daughter was up to, snagged her around the waist and snuggled her close. "I think you need to be punished."

"No, Mommy! No!" Madison giggled with anticipation.

"Sorry, but you're in big trouble now." Laughing, too, she kissed her baby's plump cheek with a smacking kiss.

"No-ooo!" Madison screeched in delight.

"One kiss." Danielle smooched the other cheek. "Two kisses."

"Mom-meeeee!" Madison giggled uncontrollably.

"Three kisses." The tip of the nose. The middle of her forehead. "Four kisses, and you know what that means."

"No tummy tickle!" The little girl squealed with glee, wiggling.

Danielle gave only the lightest of tickles, warm with happiness to the tips of her toes as her daughter wiggled and laughed.

"All right, what's going on in here?" Jonas filled the doorway, dressed in his running shoes and sweats, ready for his early-morning physical therapy appointment.

"Daddy! Mommy's kissin' me."

"Is that right? I'm afraid I can't let this go on." He came into the room, moving quickly with his cane, grinning ear to ear. "Not without me."

"No! Daddy! No-ooo—" Madison's protest dissolved into more happy squeals as Jonas gave her a loud smacking kiss on her cheek.

Why did he have to be so wonderful? Danielle felt her heart take a long slow glide, falling again, for this man. Love she could not stop. Love that had no beginning or end. Love that made her see Jonas from the past, taking precious time with his daughter. Love that made her see this new Jonas, enamored with their little girl.

Love wasn't a sum of every past moment of shared history. She hadn't realized that before, because she had always thought that it was their devotion to one another, day by day, that built upon itself to make their marriage a strong one.

But as Madison wrapped her arms around her father and laughed when he blew a raspberry against her throat, making her howl and squirm with delight, Danielle knew he didn't remember the morning Madison came into the world, all pink and fresh and new. He didn't remember how he'd been the one who could make her stop crying. That he was the one she called for when she was scared.

But being unable to remember hadn't diminished his love for his child.

"Hey!" Tyler tromped into the room and wrapped his arms around his dad's knees. "Do you know what? Today's the perfect day for getting *something*."

A dog. Danielle ruffled her fingers through Tyler's hair and gave Jonas a warning look. "Don't even think it."

His eyes glimmered at her. "I don't know. It could be a good day for getting something."

"Jonas—" Oh, she could see how this was. "You two are teaming up against me."

Tyler gasped. "So, can we do it? Can we get a dog?"

"I wanna dog!" Madison added, never to be left out of a conversation.

Danielle sighed. A dog. She had her hands more than full as it was, and yet one look at Tyler's wide, pleading eyes—oh, he knew how to work her—and then at Jonas's quieter, more serious request, all the reasons why now wasn't the right time faded into none at all.

"All right." She said those fateful words, hardly getting the last one out before Tyler shouted in triumph and Jonas gave her a loud smacking kiss on the cheek, just as he'd done to Madison. It made the kids laugh, but there was something else, just beneath the surface, that lurked like shadows in Jonas's eyes.

This was important to him and Lord help her, she'd never been able to say no to the man. The man she now loved more, impossibly more, for how hard he had fought to come back to her.

Their past no longer mattered. Love was so much more than where they had been or where they were going.

It was where they were. Together.

Danielle had never imagined the heartbreak in the eyes of the rows and rows of kennels at the local shelter. Big dogs, little dogs, in-between dogs, all with big soulful eyes. From the moment the kids stepped foot in the aisle, nearly all the dogs raced to the front of their cages, offering friendly pants to excited yips to "look at me!" barks.

Jonas's hand settled on her shoulder. "How are we ever going to pick?"

"I don't know. It means saying no to all but one of them." She knew next to nothing about dogs, but she liked them well enough. Grandpop, when he'd been alive, always had a dog. There certainly seemed to be so many nice ones, like the big yellow dog pressed against the metal cage, trying to get his tongue on Madison's head.

"Stay with me, sweetie." She held on to her daughter's little hand firmly. "We don't want to startle any of the dogs."

"They love me, Mom." Madison pulled hard, trying to get free. "Look at the curly one!"

A white curly-haired dog panted, as if trying to make friends.

"Look at the chocolate one!"

In the kennel next door, a brown dog danced happily, trying to steal the attention.

"Mom!" A few steps ahead, Tyler stood in the middle of the aisle, contemplating all his options. "Mom! That's the one!"

His loudness seemed an invitation for all the dogs to make more noise. And as the barks echoed and a caretaker ordered them to hush, Tyler went down on his knees in front of a center cage, with his hand out. A white nose pressed against his palm and licked happily.

"He's polka-dotted!" Madison gave a mighty yank, and her sticky fingers slid out of Danielle's grip and raced over to her big brother.

"Mom!" Tyler was pink with delight. "This is him. It's Lucky!"

A long list of why this might not be the dog rolled into her head and onto the tip of her tongue, but Jonas's grip on her shoulder tightened just a touch.

"Let me," he said in that resolute way of his, limping over to the children and the dog who was doing his best to win everyone's affections.

Jonas had been raised with dogs, so she trusted him to know if this was a thoroughly gentle creature. He knelt down with some difficulty and began rubbing what he could of the dog's head through the metal barrier. "Aw, you're just a good guy, aren't you?"

The dog, pure white sprinkled with black dots, panted happily and licked Jonas's nose.

"I love him." Tyler sighed with contentment, his mind—no, his heart—made up.

"Mommy! He licked my hand." Madison rubbed her palm against her rosebud-sprinkled T-shirt to dry it off, but she was pink with joy.

Four pairs of eyes turned to her, all powerfully pleading. No words were necessary. Not a single one. From Tyler's heart-deep pleading to Madison's delight to Jonas's silent nod to her, she felt her resistance buckle. Even the dog pleaded with her silently, big friendly eyes that were filled with too much sadness.

She had enough on her plate without falling in love with a dog—thankyouverymuch, as Rebecca would say.

Thirty-five minutes later Danielle was in the minivan driving toward home with all four of them in the van—plus the dog, collapsed on the floor at Tyler's feet, yipping, his voice rising and falling, as if he were talking excitedly.

"Boy, he's sure glad to have me for a best friend," Tyler commented as he petted the Dalmatian's head.

"Mommy!" Madison shrieked, giggling. "He licked my toes. It tickles. Ahhhhh!!"

Jonas, behind the wheel, flashed her a telling glance and spoke over the yip and yap of the dog's chatter. "At least she's forgotten to scream about the seat belt. See, the dog is a good thing already."

Madison squealed again, and the dog vocalized even louder.

"Yes," Danielle said, fighting not to laugh. "I can see how things have changed. Any louder, and the cops will pull us over and ticket us for breaking city decibel ordinances. We're louder than a truck downshifting on a steep hill."

Jonas laughed. "There's Mr. Paco's Tacos. How about we pick up a celebration lunch?"

"Sure." The ham-and-cheese sandwiches she'd planned for lunch sounded a little drab.

When they swung through the drive-through, Tyler insisted on an extra taco for Lucky—who knew what would be the consequence of that? And the dog's tail thumped continuously from the moment he smelled the bagged food.

"Homeward," Jonas said, as he pulled out into traffic. "Unless there is anywhere else the lady wants to go?"

"Oh, I can think of a few places," she quipped. "Some place really quiet. Maybe Fiji. I could see Aubrey and William."

"You'd miss the kids before the plane got off the ground." Jonas smiled at her, impossibly handsome even with his lopsided grin.

"True. There's no other place I'd rather be."

"Me, either."

He stopped for a red light and for a long moment, his gaze met hers with unashamed intensity. Sweetness filled her. It was good to be with her husband with the kids in the back—a real family again.

When she glanced over her shoulder at the little ones, they both looked like the happiest children on earth. But not as happy as the Dalmatian, who drooled all over the upholstery.

"You lucked out, you know that," she said to the dog and couldn't help patting his head. His short hair was warm and velvety, and he pressed ardently against her touch. It was impossible not to adore him.

"When we get home, Mom," Tyler began, talking a mile a minute over Madison's squealing and the dog's vocalizing, "can I take Lucky and show him my room? It's his room now, too, and he's gonna sleep with me so he should see it. We're best friends, you know. Do you think he'll like tacos? I hope so, cuz I do. And Tater Tots. And cookies. Then after lunch, I'm gonna show him—"

And so it went all the way home.

Why was it that whatever you were seeking was always in the very last place you looked? Danielle snatched the camera out of the back of her craft closet, not even remembering how it had gotten there. When was the last time she'd used it? Oh, for Madison's second birthday in early December. Christmas last year had been spent in Seattle, and she had forgotten to bring it. That had been a tough holiday, with her family so far away and Jonas in a wheelchair. They had only stayed with him a few hours between the kids' exhaustion from traveling and the clinic's visiting hours. The upside had been that the kids never had the chance to figure out their father didn't know them.

Maybe it had been best she didn't have any pictures from that time in their lives, she thought, overcome with pain for them all. The shouts and squeals from the backyard drifting through the open window reminded her that better times had come back to them. God was gracious, indeed.

With camera in hand, she went to check the battery—and hoped it wasn't dead—it was very low. Great. She went back through the closet looking for the plug-in and what did she find sitting next to it on the shelf? The stacks of pictures and half-done scrapbook pages she kept meaning to finish. She brought them out onto her work desk.

The phone rang, echoing through the upstairs, and the downstairs phone jingled in unison. She went to the desk, camera and charger in hand, and picked up the receiver. "Hello?"

"Dani?" Katherine's voice came across the line, sounding much better. "You called me twice, and I'm finally getting back to you."

"You've been on my mind and in my prayers, but first Mom called during breakfast with a report on how you were doing. Lauren called when I was finishing up the breakfast dishes and then Ava called around ten, caught me on my cell when we were on the road."

"Glad everyone kept you informed. Then you know I'm doing better. Were you on your way to another one of Jonas's appointments?"

"No. Guess what we got?" Danielle plugged in the camera. "Something Tyler has been begging for for a while now."

"A dog. That must mean things are getting back to normal for you guys. You and Jonas deserve to be happy again. It wasn't fair what happened to him. It wasn't right."

"No, but sometimes life is like that. No one is immune to it. And Jonas is going to be fine." Maybe not the same, but fine. Danielle's gaze found him automatically. He was in sight of the window, outside with the kids, throwing a tennis ball for Lucky. The kids clapped and hopped in place with excitement. Their blissful sounds drifted in like the sunlight and made her soul ache with gratitude. "I know it will be all right. God is in charge."

"He is," Katherine agreed. "Do you want to know some scoop?"

"Ooh, do I." Danielle slid into a nearby chair, keeping the window in sight. Jonas was calling advice to Lucky, who wasn't sure he wanted to bring back the ball he'd run so far to catch. "Is this family scoop, or your news?"

"My news. Well, Jack's and mine and Hayden's. I had another ultrasound and this time I couldn't resist. I had to know. We're having a little boy."

"A boy." Danielle sighed the words. "Congratulations. That is good news."

"The best. Jack's about fit to burst, he's so proud, and Hayden can't wait for him to get here. I've been home in bed for only a few days and I'm going nuts. I miss work. I miss puttering in my roses. I miss fixing dinner with Jack now that he's gone to day shift."

"I can come over and keep you company whenever you want."

"I'm counting on it. I'll let you go back to your handsome husband and kids. This is time you don't want to waste with them."

"Yes. I know how quickly it can change."

"It changes anyway. Time passes, there's no stopping it. So, just enjoy your family. I'll talk to you tomorrow."

"That's a promise. Call anytime if you need me." After Katherine promised to, they said goodbye. Danielle hung up and unwound the knot in the cord. The kids were at the far side of the fenced yard, trying to convince Lucky to give up the tennis ball, but he was having none of it. His tail wagged furiously as he ran a few feet, then stopped so both kids would wrap their arms around him and squeeze him with hugs, laughing the whole while. Jonas limped a few feet closer, watching over them. Awash in sunlight with his dark hair tousled by the hot puff of wind, he looked like more than the man she'd fallen in love with—iron-strong and twice as good at heart.

She tried to tell herself it didn't hurt that he couldn't yet love her back, but it did hurt. Very much. She longed for him to sense her gaze, the way he used to. They were so in tune to one another, but that was mostly gone now. She was content watching her husband playing with the kids. Love and laughter shaped his chiseled, granite face.

At least he loves them. Lord, I am deeply grateful for that. They were good kids, and easy to love. Already the dog was smitten with them, too, as he finally dropped the ball to give Tyler a big kiss on the top of his head.

Madison squealed, "E-eeew!" but raced up, wanting the same treatment and laughed when Lucky obliged.

Jonas went down on his knees next to the kids and put his arms around the dog's neck. The Dalmatian wiggled and pranced, as if happy beyond bearing.

Danielle lifted the camera, flipped off the lens cover and framed the shot. She saw raw emotion in Jonas's face. She saw gratitude. She snapped and caught the image forever of the protective dad laughing with his kids, his heart in his eyes.

It wasn't fair that her love went on. Every day growing a little bigger and deepening a little more. But love was like that—beyond all reason and more than what made a person feel safe.

Since there was enough juice in the battery to last for a little while, she took it with her on the way to the sliding door. Standing in the shadows beneath the overhead deck and watching her family, she felt alone. Tyler had turned on the water, and it arced from the sprinkler set in the middle of the lawn.

"Wroor! Wroor!" Lucky's bark was one of sheer joy as he leaped headfirst into the spray, thereby winning Tyler's heart forever. The little boy joined him. They stood in the middle of the sprinkler, battered by the sparkling rainbows of water until they were both drenched.

Madison watched on the sidelines, hanging on to her daddy's hand, alternating between taking one step toward them and back, shouting, "Wait! Tyler!"

Tyler took off on the far side of the lawn. "Come on, Lucky. Follow me."

Madison's irritation flared. "Tyler! You wait!"

Jonas knelt to whisper something in his daughter's ear, and she gazed up at him adoringly. The red temper eased from her face. Side by side, it was easy to see how much she resembled her daddy, too. She had his dimpled chin and cowlick at the crown of her head. She had his smile. Without thinking, Danielle lifted the camera to capture the image of father and daughter, hand in hand.

"Dani!" Jonas spotted her. He bent to say something else to Madison and put something in her hand.

What was going on? Danielle could tell by the mischief on the little girl's face as she ran around the spray of water on her pretty new pink sandals—perhaps the reason she wasn't running circles through the sprinkler.

"Mommy." She held out a small white envelope. "Here."

"Is this from Daddy?"

"Yip. Tyler was s'posed to give it to you, but I git to." She preened, adorable.

"Thank you. You are the best girl ever."

"Yip." As if she'd heard that one too many times, Madison gave a beleaguered sigh. It was hard being the best girl ever, apparently. "Mommy, I wanna sprinkle, too!"

"All right." She set the camera aside and unbuckled the new shoes. The straps were still a little too stiff for Madison's fingers, so she helped her out of them.

Madison raced off, bare feet pattering against the cement patio and then muffled in the lush grass. She shouted after Tyler. Lucky leaped and frolicked when she joined them.

Jonas was watching her over the heads of the children and the sparkling sprinkler water. His gaze was steady and watchful and tender—impossibly tender.

Her hands trembled as she opened the flap and pulled out the note written on lined notebook paper.

Jonas had written, *Six o'clock Friday. Prepare to be lifted off your feet.*

She had to read it twice, her heart pounding. Friday. Their anniversary. He'd remembered. She only had to look up and see the answer on his face. He was coming her way, the metal of his cane glinting in the sunlight and his step more sure. His nearness was a blessing that bridged the emotional distance between them.

"Who told you this time?" she asked, unable to hide her pleasure or, she supposed, her excitement.

"Between your mom, Katherine and Ava, I think I got the real scoop." He gave her his full-fledged, all-out-dimpled grin, the one that had always charmed her.

Oh, he had her, heart and soul. She did her best to hide it. He was under enough pressure as it was. "You mean you grilled Katherine, when she was just home from the hospital?"

"Guilty. She seemed awfully happy to tell me what she knew about our third date. So did your mom."

"Mom? Poor Mom. I don't know what she could contribute, since I kept her in the dark a lot. You know, I was afraid it wouldn't work out."

"You mean you were afraid because you doubted me?"

"Doubt you?" Her heart would stop beating before that ever happened. "No. I doubted myself. I was afraid to believe that this could work out. You were so w-wonderful. You are."

How could she be flustered like this after almost eight years of marriage? How could it feel the same as it did when they were dating? Her palms were damp, her skin itchy with nerves, her pulse quivering, and beneath all that hope was a terrible dark well of fear. Love, she knew, didn't always work out.

Sometimes, even happy marriages failed.

Jonas took her hand, the paper she held crinkled, but it was his soul she saw in the dark intensity of his eyes. "I'm not the wonderful one. You blow me away, Dani. I'm not the man you married. I'm not taking care of you or providing for my family—"

"You did those things when you were well, Jonas."

"I know. And I will do them again. What I'm saying is a lot of women would be resentful or angry. Some women might take a look at their husband leaning on a cane with his hand gnarled up and bail. But not you."

"You are making me into something I'm not. I love you. That's what love is."

"I see that." He reached out with his hand, his fingertips grazing her cheek. It was not only tenderness in his touch as he caressed her skin. "Do you remember when I first came out of the coma? When I opened my eyes?"

"Do I. That was everything I had been praying for."

"I was thinking, wow, who is that gorgeous woman and how did I get so blessed to have her sitting at my side?"

"You, sir, are fibbing."

"No, I'm telling the honest truth."

"I was a mess. I sat day and night with you. Who knows the last time I had brushed my hair. I had horrible bruises beneath my eyes. It was a wonder that I didn't scare you back into that coma."

She doesn't know, Jonas realized, dumbfounded and touched all at once. After all their years together, she did not know exactly what he saw when he looked at her. His chest tightened with regret. With disappointment in himself. What had been wrong with him that he had hadn't made sure she knew that every single day of their marriage? "You are my wife. You are the most beautiful sight in the world to me."

"Oh, Jonas." She waved away his compliment, blushing, uncomfortable.

He could see that, too. Humility was a good thing, but a wife should believe in her husband's commitment to her. "The next best are those kids right there. You are, like they are, my world, Dani. Now, more than ever."

There were no words to tell her she was the reason he stood before her, trying to bare his heart, trying to be the man she loved. Hoping there was a chance she could love the man he was now even more.

Her hand covered his, as soft as warm silk, as welcome as the rarest grace. His heart caught like an engine roaring to life. His soul filled with rare, powerful tenderness he could not quantify. He didn't need to. Love was filling him up, and it was because of her. Danielle was doing this to him. She was bringing his heart to life.

"Hey!" a man's voice called out over the sound of the kids and the running water.

The dog yapped with crazy excitement, racing over to the open gate where Spence stood in a grass-stained pair of shorts and a T-shirt. He reached out to rub the dog's head. "You're a good boy, aren't you, buddy?"

The rare moment was broken, but not gone. Jonas twined his fingers with Dani's and turned to welcome his brother-in-law, who was already surrounded by the dog and the kids.

"We'd better go rescue Spence," Dani said, moving away from him, her hand leaving his.

It was amazing how she took his heart with her, as if she'd owned it all along.

Chapter Twelve

As it turned out, Spence wasn't alone. Rebecca had come with him driving Jonas's truck, which sat sparkling clean and waxed in the driveway. They had stayed for supper, and the men were outside with the kids and the dog, while she and Rebecca were doing the cleanup.

Now that she was finally alone with her little sister, Danielle rinsed the sponge at the sink and asked what had been troubling her. "Something is wrong. Spence hasn't said anything and neither have you, but I can tell. It's not like you spend a lot of time hanging with Spence."

"He, ah, thought I shouldn't sit home alone." Rebecca was busy stacking the dishwasher and didn't look up.

She seemed alone and somehow fragile. Danielle left the sponge on the counter and laid a hand on her sister's shoulder. Something was definitely wrong. "More trouble with Chris?"

"Trouble? No. Not anymore."

There was nothing but tension in the girl's shoulder. Nothing but misery in her voice. Danielle's stomach bunched up tight. Something wasn't just wrong; it was *really* wrong. "What happened, Becca?"

"I didn't know how to tell anyone this, but Chris showed up again."

Maybe it was the tremor in her little sister's voice that kept her silent, and she waited, not daring to say a thing. She dearly hoped this didn't mean things were back on with the boyfriend. "Did he want to get back together with you?"

"He did, but I d-didn't. He got pretty angry. Real angry. I d-didn't think he would take it so h-hard."

There were a thousand things Danielle wanted to say—mostly that Rebecca deserved a great man, a perfect man, one who would see all the lovely qualities and gifts in her. But she again kept silent. She searched for the understanding her baby sister needed. "He seems like a man who has a lot of personal problems."

The happy sounds from the backyard drifted through the open windows. The joyful Ruff! Ruff! of the dog. The kids' high voices and musical giggles. The low rumble as Jonas laughed along with them.

Rebecca took a shaky breath. "It's over now. Spence made sure of that for me."

"Do you mean Chris got violent?"

"I don't know if it would have come to that. He was pretty enraged. I called Spence and he came over and settled it. The next time he shows up, I'm pressing charges."

"And why didn't you do it this time?"

"Because everyone deserves a chance to put their lives together, and he didn't hurt me. He just yelled."

As if that wasn't abusive enough. Danielle hated this. She hated what her sister was going through. "Are you safe?"

"I'm fine. See? This is why I shouldn't have told you. You're going to worry. You're going to confide in everyone else in the family, and the next thing everyone will know what a f-fool I'd been. Believing in something I wanted so badly, and it wasn't true."

"Maybe it was what Chris wanted for himself, but wasn't man enough to stand up for." Danielle thought of Jonas. No matter what, he had always been the kind of man who stood for what was right, no matter how tough that was. He was a man she could put all her trust in—always had and always would.

If only she wasn't so lonesome for Jonas's glance across a room, for that secret smile they would share when they knew they had the same thought. For the strengthening comfort of his touch.

"You shouldn't go back to your place tonight." Danielle thought of the spare bedroom downstairs. "Why don't you stay over? You can stick around and see exactly how house-trained Lucky is."

"No, I'll leave that special joy to you." Rebecca swiped her eyes, trying to make light of things. "He seems so gentle. Do you know his background?"

"He had too much energy for the working couple who had him, at least that was according to his paperwork at the shelter. He's been known to chew furniture, so I've got my eye on him. We'll see what other surprises come with him."

"Good ones, I think. He's so good with the kids."

"His saving grace, whatever he does to the rest of the house." Danielle didn't add that she was already a little smitten with the big lovable guy. Anyone who was so sweet to her children had an in with her. She went back to wiping down the counter, keeping an eye on her sister. "Don't worry. The right man will come along, you just wait. Then you'll see that God had a better path in mind for you all along."

"No, I'm firmly sticking to my No Man policy. Although if I ever break it, I hope I wind up as lucky as you and Jonas."

Jonas. Simply at the thought of him, love filled her with radiance. Longing filled her, too—for his closeness, his love. She was lonely for him. She was afraid that would never change. That they'd come as far as they could toward one another.

"Dani? You look so pale all of a sudden." Becca looked up from loading the last of the cups. Worry lined her dear face. "Do you need to sit down?"

"No, I'm fine." On the outside, anyway. Maybe that was why she felt as if she were going down for the third time—because she had had the most wonderful day with her husband and kids. They'd had a good day, just like they used to always have.

But at the end of this day, there would be no snuggling with Jonas on the couch. No loving glances over the children's heads. No waiting until Madison finally gave in to sleep, for their time alone.

This isn't helping, Danielle. She blew out a breath, resolving to think of the good in this day. This wonderful, precious day the Lord had given them. She should not fill it with regret.

"You don't look all right." Rebecca abandoned the dishwasher to come closer. "You're not pregnant, are you?"

"Pregnant? No. I'm not." She gripped the edge of the counter, feeling the wave take her over and wash her away.

Painful loneliness left her without breath. She felt lost, so desperately lost. She might have his support and his concern, but she did not have his love as her anchor.

Rebecca was watching her with such hopeful anticipation, as if she'd guessed a new secret. Danielle faltered. How could she admit that her husband hadn't so much as kissed her? That every night he'd fallen asleep before she had finished brushing her teeth? How could she find the strength to say the truth: that her beloved Jonas did not want her? That he did not love her in return?

"Dani, are you sure? Then you've got to be really tired. You're worn-out. You've pushed yourself so hard over the last year. Maybe it's time to take it a little easier. Go sit down, put your feet up. I'll finish here. Go on."

"I'm not leaving you with my work."

"It's the least I can do for feeding me." She snatched the dishrag from the counter and continued on with the wiping down.

That Rebecca. She had a stubborn streak. Bless her.

Jonas's uneven gait rang in the hallway, the sounds from outside of laughing children and Lucky's occasional woof drifting after him. Jonas was drenched, as if he'd taken a few turns in the sprinkler, too, and it looked as if it had done him good.

"I let the kids talk me into getting them a Popsicle each." His grin was wide and captivating.

Riveted, she could not look away. Why hadn't she noticed before how his smile was no longer as lopsided? Laughter lifted him up, and he stood tall and substantial as if nothing could ever hurt him again. Just when she thought she couldn't adore him any more, her heart swelled a little more.

"A Popsicle?" Her feet took her closer to him without thought. Her spirit leaned toward his without intention. "I suppose I could deliver them. What would be in it for me?"

"Besides my eternal gratitude? Well, let's see. I suppose you could keep a Popsicle for yourself."

"As if that's motivation enough?"

"Two Popsicle treats?"

She shook her head. "I think seeing my husband and kids so happy is more than enough. I'll hit the freezer and be right down."

"I'll wait for you. You might need a bodyguard. Popsicle treats are valuable, and I wouldn't want you to be waylaid. Nope, I'd best stick close to you, just in case."

"I suppose that's a good idea." Bliss lifted her right off the ground. "We wouldn't want anything to happen to the Popsicle treats. I'll go get them."

After Spence and Rebecca left, it had taken quite a bit of effort to get the kids settled down, bathed and in bed for the night. Madison had finally drifted off over one of her favorite storybooks, and there had been cleanup and laundry to do. The kids had used every towel in the house, or so it seemed. And since Jonas was reading to Tyler, she'd taken the chance to sit down at the table with a cup of tea and catch up on her devotional reading.

She focused on the page, going over one of her favorite verses—okay, she had many favorite verses. *I wait for the Lord, my soul waits, and in his word I put my hope.*

See? She might be lonely for Jonas, but she had to have more patience and give God more time to work in their lives. Already He had done so much for them.

Danielle leaned back in the chair, knowing she had been so busy that she hadn't done as much as she could for the Lord. She regretted that. Now that life was settling down, maybe she and Jonas could start going back to their regular Bible study. Maybe she would speak with Spence about volunteering for one of his many committees. He was so active in the church charities.

"You and Rebecca sure looked serious." Jonas's baritone came out of the darkness. He eased into sight through the kitchen toward the light. There was something in his eyes—something intimate and caring—which made her heart stall.

Jonas had something in his arms—it looked like books. No, more picture albums. She set aside her Bible, her devotional reading done, sitting straighter in her chair. "Rebecca has not been as fortunate as I was with her first boyfriend."

Jonas's eyebrow quirked as he approached the table. "I was your first boyfriend."

"Yes, you were, handsome. I'll always be grateful to you that you made sure I didn't push you away."

"Because I frightened you." He nodded slowly, his voice falling a note. "You were afraid of getting hurt."

"I was afraid of losing you." *I still am.* She held that back, too, another secret between them. "Think of what would have happened that day we met if you made a different decision about me."

"Seems to me you were the one who accepted me." He slid the books on the edge of the table, looking thoughtful and somber in the meager fall of light. "I can't imagine where I would be if you hadn't let me come into your life. I wish I could remember that day, the day everything changed. It was the day that has brought me here, right here, with you."

Jonas, her dear Jonas. Emotion gathered behind her eyes, hurting and sweet all at once. She was overwhelmed by this man, as she had been so many times before. By his kindness, his honesty and his depth of feeling. She wished he would come closer and draw her into his arms. Let her lean against him. She needed his love.

"I hope your sister's going to be all right." He settled into the chair across from her, the table separating them. "Tyler's finally asleep. He had a hard time settling down, what with the dog in his room."

"That dog." Danielle shook her head, fondly going over the events of the evening. The dog had pranced around the barbecue grill, so excited by the thought of those hamburgers and hot dogs grilling away. He'd sat down on the bench at the picnic table, as if he were a little boy and not a dog. Then he sat on the ground beside the picnic table with his own plate—yes, he got his own hot dog—on the floor in front of him. The plate had been Madison's idea. "Something tells me we might be the lucky ones."

"He's a good guy, and we can trust him with the kids." Jonas opened one album cover. "He'll be a good friend to Tyler."

"Especially since he loves to play in water, too." The backyard was probably still an inch deep in pooled water from the kids playing all through the evening. "Is that Tyler's book?"

"Right now I'm looking at pre-Tyler." Jonas blushed a little.

Danielle leaned in her chair to get a glimpse. "I was eight and a half months pregnant right there. See those new sandals? I couldn't see my feet."

Jonas tapped the snapshot. "I took this."

"Yes," she agreed. She had been caught in the act of smiling at her beloved husband as he'd snapped the picture. "We were at Gran's house for Tyler's baby shower. I remember Ava made a cake in the shape of a baby bassinet and dozens of colorful iced cookies shaped like baby rattles. and shoes. If you turn the page, you'll see them."

"What I see is you." Jonas tapped another picture.

"I was pretty big then. I was hard to miss." She was joking. He was not. "You're beautiful."

"You have to say that. You're my husband."

"No. It's the truth." To him, it was more than the truth. She looked radiant, luminous, and she'd been his. His bride, his wife, the woman carrying his unborn child. Rare tenderness tore him up like a blade, took him down and left him in pieces.

I wish I remembered. A prayer lifted up from the depths of his soul. *Please, Lord, show me the way back to her.*

It seemed just a short distance, after all, since she was across the table from him, within reach. All he had to do was to touch her hand with his to close the physical distance.

It was the emotional distance he did not know how to cross. They had a bond, him and Dani, as plain to see as the images before him. How every look she sent him in those pictures held a message, a secret that only the old Jonas could decipher. Every smile that touched her lips had meaning, one he used to understand, for the same smile would be mirrored on his face.

How did they that find that closeness again? Maybe, he thought, when he was whole again. He sure longed for it. He could see the way they leaned toward one another, whether they were across a room or next to one another on the couch. It was in the link of their gazes, as if they only saw each other, as if the entire world had ceased to exist for that moment, that touch, that kiss.

Jonas turned the page, transfixed by the look of love on his own face. By his arm lying easily across her shoulders, hugging her to him. By the way she tilted her head back to gaze up at him in a long, still look. Adoration, devotion, he didn't know what to call it, but it made Danielle beyond beautiful. It made her his.

How did he get there from here? He did not know.

Her soft alto drew him away from his thoughts.

"I was having a terrible hair day then, kind of like today." Self-conscious, she ran a hand over her rich brown locks that curled every which way at the ends. "Turn the page. That's when Dad and Spence helped you haul everything into the nursery. Look at all of that! We had so many friends and family—including the huge shower our church group had for us. We hardly had any space left in the room."

So many friends and family. Church friends and family he could not remember, either. These were the people who came up to him whenever he was out—Lucy at the bookstore. Mark at the restaurant. And others when he had been getting out of the van at the animal shelter. At the physical therapy office. Before and after Sunday morning service. These people were the ones Dani and her family talked about who had brought by casseroles when she'd been at the hospital for the kids, who had put on car washes and bake sales and fund-raisers to raise money on his behalf— Dani had donated the proceeds to the troopers' widows and orphans fund.

Overwhelmed, he tried to concentrate on the pictures in front of him, but it was tough. How many people had he forgotten? Not only his wife and kids, but his friends? People who had mattered to him? It was as if he'd only just realized he'd lost more than half of his memories.

He'd lost half of his life. It was gone, forever out of his reach. He was glad to be here, he was glad for God's grace in allowing him to live, but how could one bullet steal so much from a man?

"And here—" Dani reached over to turn the page. "Look at this. The look on your face as you were driving me to the hospital. My water had broken and you were in a total panic. I had to get a picture of you, and you didn't think I was one bit funny, buster."

There was no mistaking the expression of panic on his own younger face. A face unmarked by nerve damage. It wasn't hard to see why he had been so afraid. Sometimes things went wrong, and Danielle—his heart stalled—she would have been a lot to lose. "I was scared for you."

"I know, handsome. But everything went like clock-work—very slow clockwork—but without a single com-plication." Her soft eyes searched his face lovingly. "You stayed with me the whole time. You were my rock. We decided on a name while I was waiting to dilate, which took forever. Look."

He turned the page and there he was, holding newborn

Tyler in the delivery room. His son. His soul sighed, and without a single memory he felt it all over again. The surge of undying devotion. A wave of love so strong it rendered him helpless and powerful all at once. He would forge any stream, leap any mountain, do anything for his son. For his wife. His family.

With every turn of the page, his affection grew. Pictures of the family visiting Dani and Tyler in the hospital. Snapshots of them heading home. Of them arriving with tiny baby Tyler. Of the exhaustion on their faces as they each took turns rocking the baby, praying he would fall asleep. Priceless images of Tyler's wee button face asleep, his little hands relaxed, utter perfection. Love blazed anew for his son. This was more than a lifetime commitment—it was for an eternity and a day.

He closed the book and saw the woman across from him in a new light.

"Jonas," she said softly. "It's after eleven. Way past our bedtime. Come with me."

He heard the love in her voice and felt it in the air between them. He longed to take her hand and to start where they'd left off. Except he was afraid.

"Later," he said, reaching for the next book. A pink one, with Madison's picture on the front cover. "You look exhausted, Dani. Go on to bed. I'll be there in a while."

She withdrew her hand, quietly as always, impossible to read as she set her chin. She smiled at him—was it a little sad?—and said in that gentle way of hers, "Don't stay up too late."

"Not too late," he agreed. He'd said the wrong thing, he realized. But what?

"You need your rest to keep healing, Jonas."

True, but he had so much work to do. So much to prove and to come back from. He had to be the man she needed. The man she loved. There was nothing on earth he wanted more than to be that man for her. He could not risk her rejecting him. If he reached for her now, what if she turned away from him?

He couldn't lose her. No, it was best to wait. His gaze roamed her lovely face, so dear to him for all the loving ways she'd looked at him, and his heart slid helplessly right out of his chest. It was no longer his.

His heart was hers.

"Good night." She looked as though she had more to say but seemed to change her mind as she pushed away from the table, taking her Bible and devotional with her.

She moved like beauty, like poetry, like grace. He watched her, even when the shadows at the far end of the kitchen deepened, hiding all but the faintest trace of her. Even after she'd turned the corner and was gone from his sight, he kept listening to the faint pad of her gait. To the faint hush of their bedroom door closing. To the faint rush of water in the bathroom sink.

Love, like faith, was a strange and wonderful thing. There was nothing tangible to both, no shape or color or texture. But the feel of love was more real than anything he could see with his eyes or touch with his hands.

His heart was aching with a kind of tenderness that hurt even as it uplifted him. He blew out a shaky breath and drew in determination. All of it he could muster. He couldn't lose her. He had to keep working harder.

Much harder. He slid the next photo album squarely in

front of him. The picture on the cover—Madison's sweet button face—blinked up at him.

He hunkered down, turned the page and let the hours pass.

Chapter Thirteen

Friday afternoon was crazy, of course. She should have anticipated that, Danielle chided herself as she grabbed the phone on the run. "Hello?"

"It's Spence. Got a moment?" Typical Spence, barking out what sounded like an order when it should have been a polite question.

"I've got half a moment," she admitted as she ran out of her bedroom and down the hallway as fast as her sandals would let her, following the trail of Madison, the escapee. "Come back here, young lady!"

Madison was only a flash of pink rounding the corner and zip! out of sight.

Great. Danielle raced around the corner. "Talk fast, Spence. I'm listening."

"Want a full-time job?"

A job? Her foot missed the stair and she stumbled. Her hand flew out and snagged the handrail, saving her from a tumble down the rest of the stairs. "Are you serious?"

"Deadly. Since you don't sound thrilled, how about this? You set your own hours into the schedule. How's that?"

"It is good timing." Considering the stack of bills growing on the counter. She hurried down the stairs, catching sight of Madison pushing open the sliding door. "Let me talk it over with Jonas, but I want to take it. You knew I was going to accept it, right?"

"Yep. Only makes sense. Jonas's rehabilitation has got to be expensive, and disability insurance helps, but it isn't the same as what Jonas was making. With Katherine out, I could use the help. This might be permanent."

"I know." It was no secret that Katherine was only going to work until the baby came. Up ahead, Madison slipped through the door with a giggle. Danielle was gaining, but she was out of breath. "Spence? How about we talk this through on Sunday? You can come over for dinner after church."

"Sure. Talk to you then."

The line clicked off. Danielle squinted against the bright glare of summer sunshine and swooped down to sweep Madison off her feet in mid-stride.

"Mommeeee!" The girl squealed. "Noooooo!"

"You are trouble, bubbles." Danielle smooched Madison's cheek, hoping to offset a coming tantrum. "You're supposed to be in bed, princess."

"No! I wanna sprinkle with Lucky!" Too tired, Madison rubbed at her eyes, her voice thin and high. "Mommy! Put me down."

Danielle winked at Tyler, who had stopped watering the imaginary fire in the petunia bed to watch. Satisfied all was not too far out of the ordinary, he went back to his work while Lucky raced circles around the yard. "I think your bunny misses you. We'd better go keep Minnie company."

"No! I wanna stay with Lucky!"

"Lucky has to take a nap, too." Sooner or later, especially after running around the yard like that.

She closed the sliding door and headed up the stairs. It wasn't easy keeping hold of a struggling wiggle box, but she'd gotten the knack of it. It wasn't easy not being unduly stressed by the loud "No! Mom-meeee!"s that were shrill enough to break her eardrum and echoed in the stairwell around her. The big lurking question was if she could manage to get Madison back down to her nap and still be able to get ready for tonight's anniversary outing on time.

"Shh, baby," Danielle cooed, gently. "Tell you what. I'll read more from your favorite storybook, okay?"

"Nooo!" With a little less gusto, now. "Mommy! I want Lucky. Mommy! I don't wanna!"

"I know, baby." She started humming a song, one of Madison's favorites, reminding herself that this phase, too, would pass. She turned into Madison's room, curtains drawn against the bright sun. She eased onto the corner of the little bed.

"No! I wanna go outside, Mommy. Please?" The girl gave a tiny sob of misery.

Danielle couldn't resist holding her baby and rocking her. Madison's arms wrapped around her neck and held on. It was hard being so little.

The alarm system chirped, announcing the front door had opened. Was it Jonas already? Or Rebecca, come early? Her whole being seemed to still, straining to listen for the first sound of a step.

Rebecca, she realized, when she didn't hear the metallic thump of Jonas's cane on the tile. "Back here," she called out.

Her youngest sister appeared in the doorway, looking lovely and fresh as a summer's day with her hair pulled back in a ponytail and her backpack slung over her shoulder. "Someone's up late from her nap."

"She never went down for one." She kissed her baby's forehead, trying to soothe her, rocking her side to side. "Too much excitement going on outside."

"Oh, right. The *D. O. G.*" Becca nodded, stepping into the room, her arms out. "Let me take Madison. I am in the mood for a story. How about it, pretty girl?"

"No." Madison hiccuped. "I wanna run fast with Lucky."

"How are things going with you?" Danielle asked as she handed her daughter over.

Rebecca took Madison lovingly and snuggled her close. "Don't worry about me, not when you and Jonas have a special evening planned."

"Our anniversary. I know." Her hopes were high. How could they not be? She was getting her husband back. Her best friend. The man who owned her heart. "Oh—there he is."

"Go. I've got Madison covered." Rebecca nodded over the top of the little girl's curls. "You aren't even dressed yet."

"Almost." She had her nice pants on. Danielle looked down at her T-shirt, smudged with Madison's applesauce from lunch. All she had to do was to pull on the matching summery top and run a brush through her hair.

Jonas. He'd ran a quick errand for her—delivering a casserole and green salad for Katherine's family's supper—and now he stood in dark trousers and a matching shirt. Caught in the act of setting a vase of a dozen pink roses on the entry table, he shot her a sheepish grin, looking so handsome, so *Jonas,* she felt her breath catch. It was as if all her hopes had been answered. Her prayers heard.

She moved toward him without thought, as if her spirit led her to his side. "Hey, handsome. Are those flowers for me?"

"For my one and only." His baritone dipped low, intimate.

The distance between them felt so small. Now, if only they could keep moving toward one another. Maybe tonight, on this third date of theirs, she would capture his heart.

"No!" Madison's shout reverberated off the high ceilings. "I don't wanna story!"

There was a thump! And then the mad dash of little feet. Madison bulleted toward them, hands pumping, little pink sandals churning.

"I got her!" Rebecca, who'd smartly worn sneakers, was gaining ground on her. "Go back to your romantic stuff. No worries!"

She launched down the staircase after Madison.

Danielle opened her mouth, ready to argue, but the giggles from downstairs told her that Rebecca had caught Madison and was punishing her with kisses. "Sometimes we're more than a little goofy around here. I hope you're not about to change your mind about me."

"Not a chance, beautiful." Jonas's warm chuckle sounded like music, like life returned to her soul. "This is fun. I'm glad I'm here, Dani. I know I've missed this—you—so much."

"I've missed you, too." She went up on tiptoe to kiss his masculine-rough cheek. Sweetness filled her. A sense of rightness poured through her soul. "Give me two more minutes to finish getting ready, and then I'm all yours, handsome."

"Lucky me."

His smile made her love him that much more.

Dinner had gone perfectly, Jonas was thankful for that. And now, watching the look on his wife's face as they rose up into the sky in the basket of the hot air balloon he'd hired, he knew he'd done good, by her standards.

He'd wanted this night to be special, as he'd learned their third date was. The pressure was on—he wanted this evening to be even better the second time around. He had to win her heart again—as the man he was now. He didn't expect that to be easy work or to come quickly. It would take time. Time he was willing to spend.

Her hands, so small and white, gripped the side of the basket. "You were telling the truth. You did your research, mister."

He inched a little closer to her. "Ava told me about the dozen pink roses. Your mother told me about the nicest restaurant in town. Katherine told me about this balloon ride."

"This sounds promising." Danielle tipped her head, the strong breeze catching her hair and it fanned around her face, lifting away so that he saw her clearly, every curve, every freckle, every hope.

"She even told me something else." He blushed to think about it. Blushed because Danielle was a quality lady, and he, as a gentleman, could not imagine even now being so bold. But he could see how it had been long ago when he and Danielle had been just getting to know one another. He'd probably felt the same as right now. As if he was dangling in midair by less than the air-driven balloon. He had never felt more terrified—or more sure of anything in his life.

"What exactly did my sister tell you?"

"That tonight, the moment after the sun slips behind those amazing mountains, I'm supposed to do something monumental."

Humor warmed her eyes. "You mean like bungee jumping?"

"That was my plan," he quipped. "But I hear that last time I chose a more romantic path, and so I think I'd best stick to that for the big finale."

"Big finale. That sounds promising."

"My thought exactly." He felt shy. There was no getting around that. They'd spent dinner talking over the photo albums he'd gone through and the pictures she'd left on her downstairs desk. But it had been the talk that made him feel closer to her. It was nothing heavy, nothing significant as they talked over the events of the last few weeks. The kids. The dog. The extended family—Katherine's health and Rebecca's problems. How Gran needed more help around the farm. He'd volunteered to go out with Spence this weekend.

He felt closer to her. He concentrated on the blue beauty of the sky and the stunning lay of the Bozeman valley below. Mountains shot upward, carpeted with trees. He managed to keep his balance in the swaying basket—those hard, painful endless hours of physical therapy were paying off.

He felt fairly sure now that he understood what she needed him to be. But he didn't know how to tell Dani what mattered. How his heart was alive and bright with devotion for her. That being with her made the sky bluer, the sun brighter, and his spirit as light as the wind against them.

Thank You, Lord, for her. He didn't need the past. He didn't need a single memory because he could see her—all of her. Everything about who she was. He adored the way she gazed up at him with unabashed affection. And the way she leaned a little closer to him. The silent question in her eyes as loving as his dreams.

Somehow he had to be good enough for her. Somehow he had to gather up his courage to do what she needed. "I don't remember the past. I have to admit that the doctors are right. I'm not going to ever remember."

There. He'd said it. He waited, heart hammering in his chest, while sadness filled her eyes. They had been working under the belief that he would come back, that he would remember because she needed him to.

Now the truth was out in the open. It wasn't going to happen. Would she still want him? Or was this it? Was it over? His soul cracked at the thought. Falling straight out of the basket and hitting the ground far below would be less painful than losing her.

"I know." She sounded sad, but not shocked. She didn't move away. She didn't turn away. "But we can go on from here. We can make new memories."

Music to his soul. Relief rushed through him like the jet stream. "I will do all I can to make 'em the best," he vowed.

"I know that, Jonas."

It helped to see her trust in him there on her beautiful face. At least that was settled. He felt better about that: they would go on from here. Now that was something he *could* do.

Determined, he took her hands in his. "I might not

remember, but I know how I must have felt all those years ago standing before you just like this. My pulse is pounding, I'm so nervous I can hardly think and talk at the same time."

She smiled, her eyes going soft with affection, with humor and more hope than he could measure. He wanted to move mountains for this woman and be everything she needed.

To be the man she needed.

"One thing is very different." He paused, searching for words. "Something tells me back then I loved you more first. That I already knew the moment I saw you in the field that I was going to marry you."

"You've said that many times over the years," she reassured him. "It was love at first sight."

"No, I think it was deeper than that. It was everything at first sight. Love. Devotion. Lifelong commitment. I know I wanted to be the one man you could always count on, who would never let you down."

"Jonas. I hope you don't think that that you've done that. Not you. Not ever." Her gaze searched his with pure honesty.

She might not see how he'd failed her. How Spence had offered her a full-time job to help support the family because he could no longer do it—yet. How she'd been alone and afraid through the last year, taking care of everything including the finances, fearing she might turn out to be a widow instead of a wife. He hadn't been able to protect her and take care of her.

Yes, he believed that she truly didn't see his failures. But he did. That she loved him still meant more to him than she would ever know. "Dani, you might think this time around that you're the one who loves more."

"Jonas, I know this has been so hard for you. The kids

and I are strangers to you, and I—" She stopped, searching for words. A gust of wind swung the basket, causing a ripple of turbulence, but he was sturdier than he had been. His hand holding hers did not let go.

It's a sign, she thought since they were dangling much closer to heaven. Much closer to the future they were meant to share. She tried not to let his honesty hurt her. "I know it will take a lot of time, time you need to l-love me again."

"But you're wrong." His hand released hers to cup the side of her face, cradling her lightly. His gaze deepened and focused on her lips.

While it wasn't a declaration of love, as he'd made on their first third date, it was close enough. Joy spilled through her like the sunlight through the red sides of the gigantic balloon above them. She soaked in this precious moment—the earth and their daily troubles were far away and the sky close enough to touch. She drank in the beauty surrounding her, the weightlessness, and the surge of wind across her face. Jonas leaned closer—so close her pulse stopped and her soul stilled in anticipation. Waiting, simply waiting for the first brush of his lips to hers. For the first tenderness of his kiss.

Everything within her sighed when his lips covered hers in a warm velvet brush. Pure sweetness. Suspended between earth and sky, between their past and their future, time stood still. She was lost in his kiss, in being closer to this new Jonas than she'd ever been before.

The trouble with kissing beneath a hot air balloon was that it was tough to do for long. The wind swirled them, the basket beneath their feet bumped and swayed, and Jonas pulled away, but he didn't let her go. He held her close, the distance between them as good as gone. For that moment, as they sailed westward toward the setting sun, it felt as if they'd never been apart. As if nothing between them had ever changed. Her hope was now that this closeness would never end.

"So," he murmured against her ear. "Did I keep my word? Have I swept you off your feet?"

"Most definitely."

He might not have said the words, but she knew he was almost there. He was almost in love with her again. As they floated through a sapphire sky toward the caramel light of sunset, a prayer lifted up from her heart. *Please, let him be in love with me. I need this so much, Lord.*

The sun blazed in glory before beginning its descent behind the rugged, amethyst mountains. Answer enough, Danielle thought, letting herself lean against Jonas and savor being snug and safe in his arms once again—even in midair.

They were pulling into the garage and Danielle suspected that she still hadn't managed to touch the ground yet. Her hopes were sky-high and her heart floating because it was so full. How could it not be? Jonas's kiss lingered like the dearest memory. They were close again. And with any luck, that closeness would grow stronger as their love always did.

Joy brightened her up like the rich, creamy sunlight they'd sailed into in that big balloon. She felt as if she were still sweetly swaying. All her troubles felt very far away and so small, they hardly mattered.

What did matter—what would always matter—was the way Jonas was gazing at her with quiet, deep affection in his eyes. He loved her. He hadn't said the words yet, but they were in the air between them. In the silence as he shut off the engine and the garage door cranked shut. In his touch as he leaned closer to cup the back of her head and slant his lips to hers.

His kiss was polite and tender. His respect for her made her feel treasured—just as it always had. Tonight *was* the night. He was going to say the words she longed to hear. She wasn't lonely anymore. She wanted to be so close to him, that there was no getting closer. She wanted to be so wrapped up in his love, that all the hardship of the past year would be washed away. There would only be the two of them and their love, a great blessing she treasured more than life. And to think that he felt this way, too, healed all the aching places within her that sadness had made.

"I don't want the evening to end," he murmured against her lips, barely breaking their kiss.

There was so much emotion in his eyes, dark and deep and intimate. She brushed her fingertips along the iron edge of his jaw. It was wonderful to be alone with him. Gazing into his eyes. Feeling their silence. Feeling as if they were in sync again.

"We don't have to let it end," she told him with a smile.

He nodded once, in agreement perhaps, and gave her one more kiss. "It's getting late. We'd better go in. Rebecca must be wondering what on earth we're doing sitting in the dark garage."

Indeed the overhead light on the electric opener had blinked out. She hadn't noticed. Her heart didn't need light to see her Jonas.

He moved away, but she didn't feel alone as he got out

of the seat and circled around to open her door. Her spirit felt linked to his—where he moved, she followed. When he opened her door and she placed her hand on his, her soul sighed. She felt whole, as if they had never been broken by his injury. When she looked at him, he seemed like perfection, her one true love.

He felt that way, too, she knew. He had all but said the words. This was their anniversary. Surely he was saving the best for last.

Rebecca was waiting for them, her backpack packed, the kitchen clean and tidy, and the kids' toys picked up and put away. "Lucky's on the foot of Tyler's bed. I couldn't get him to budge."

"Join the crowd." Danielle couldn't help joking. She felt wonderful with Jonas at her side, his hand at her elbow, his presence right behind her. He was physically close, but it was much more than that—he was emotionally close, too.

She turned toward him as he reached to take her cardigan and her purse. Without a word he went to put them away for her. Across the room his gaze found hers and there was that smile, lopsided and dear, that made her heart tug, as if an invisible rope linked them. As love bound them.

She hardly noticed Rebecca until she spoke, already at the front door, her voice low to keep from waking the kids. "I'll just go. We'll catch up later. See ya."

"Uh—bye!" Too late, the door was closed, her sister was gone and she was alone with her husband. Alone, standing before him vulnerable, with her heart wide-open, waiting for the words he'd said for the first time on that long-ago third date. Needing to hear those words with all the pieces of her soul.

Jonas checked the lock on the front door and as he set the alarm for the night, his rich baritone was nothing but rumbling tenderness. "I'll check on the kids on my way to bed."

To bed? She watched, her jaw falling slack, as incredibly he took one step away from her. Then another. And another until the shadows of the hallway claimed him.

She could still feel the pull of his heart to hers and the connection of the emotions they'd shared. But this wasn't the way she needed their date to end, as if that closeness was over. As if they were in the business of marriage together, and nothing more, with a typical evening routine of checking the house and the kids. The fairy-tale-like sweetness of their date screeched to an end. Her hopes crashed to the ground.

There would be no words of endearment, no vows of love and devotion and none of the emotional closeness she craved with her beloved husband. That was it. She was at her breaking point. She'd managed to hold it together through the coma, through the shattering realization that she was a stranger to him, that long lonely stretch when he was away in Seattle and the disappointing loneliness when he'd come back home.

I need you, Jonas. She didn't know how to tell him. Hadn't she pressured him enough as it was? He feared that he was a disappointment to her—to *her.* What kind of wife was she if she couldn't inspire love in her own husband? And on their wedding anniversary, no less.

Alone in the shadows, Danielle bowed her head. Jonas's uneven gait receded down the hall, putting darkness and distance between them, as if any closeness had been nothing but her wish—and hers alone.

Chapter Fourteen

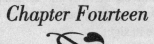

Jonas rubbed his face dry with the hand towel, feeling great about how the evening turned out. Dani had looked so happy tonight. He'd checked on both the kids and the dog, and there was nothing more for her to do. He'd done everything he could for his wife today. He hated that it wasn't enough, as it once had been.

He also hated that she felt she had to take the full-time job Spence had offered her. But before long he intended to be back at work. Not on regular patrol—probably never again with his leg, but he would be glad to go back to his desk, managing troopers and shuffling papers.

Soon, he promised himself. He would work hard enough to make that happen, no matter how painful those dreaded physical therapy appointments were. He wiped up the splashes around the sink—he still made a lot—and hung the towel. There. Nothing left to do but to say his prayers, and that was a long list these days. He had so much to be thankful for. God had allowed him to come back to this life—and it was a good one.

He grabbed his cane and limped into the bedroom. His leg was bothering him a lot. The balloon ride hadn't been easy. He'd used his leg too much trying to keep his balance, but it had been for a good cause. Dani and he had moved one step closer.

Speaking of his wife, where was she? The bedroom door was open into the hallway and the lamp he'd left on by the bed glowed brightly, but there was no Dani. She wasn't anywhere in sight.

Maybe she'd treated herself to some tea and some downtime. He yanked open the top dresser drawer for his pj's and that's when he heard it, the soft snuffling sound of a muffled sob. His heart fell to the floor. Was that Dani? He was hardly aware of getting out of the room and down the hall, past the kids' closed doors. Suddenly he was in the kitchen, frozen in place, staring with disbelief.

His Dani sat with her hands in her face at the table, her shoulders shaking. He'd never seen anyone cry so silently. Tears rolled between her fingers to drip onto the polished wood. She was hurting. She was in pain—his wife. Why? She was crying as if she'd lost everything in the world, and she muffled another racking sob. He felt her agony like a tsunami crashing into him, as if knocking him to his feet.

What was wrong? Why was she hurting like this? He took one step closer, and he knew. He'd failed her. This was what she'd been hiding from him, what he'd feared all along. He wasn't the man he was. She knew it; he knew it and it was hurting her with an agony she'd been shouldering alone.

He went to her. Heaven knew nothing was worse than facing his failure to this woman—this woman who was the reason he found strength to breathe every morning. This woman, who was the reason he fought so hard every day. Her love was what had driven him before in that life he could not remember—and it drove him now.

"Jonas." She looked up, startled, when he came out of the darkness. Tears streaked her face. Her eyes were glassy and her nose red, but she was still his beautiful Danielle, his treasured wife.

Sadness shadowed her and, seeing that raw torment, he went down on both knees. He'd done this to her. He hadn't meant to. He'd given everything he had to come back to her. What if it wasn't enough?

"J-Jonas." She swiped at her face, turning away as if to hide from him. As if she was ashamed.

He caught her hands, wet from her tears and so cold, as if an indicator of her sorrow. He prayed hard for the right words. "I thought everything was going well tonight. Why are you crying?"

"I'm not. I'm stopping." More tears rolled down her face, as if against her will.

He knew what this was about. The issue they had talked around. The issue she had stoutly denied. But it was too huge to ignore anymore. "Dani, I'm not the man I was, and I know this is hard on you."

"Jonas, this is not about your injury."

"Yes, it is. You have to know—" His voice broke. "You've got to know that things are going to get better. I promise you."

"Oh, Jonas. This isn't that—" She hiccuped and turned away, swiveling in the chair, until all he could see was the line of her neck, the curve of her hunched shoulder and the shine of tears on her cheek.

She took a wobbly breath, as if she were fighting more tears. "I know things are going to get better. This is so stupid of me. Forgive me. Just f-for-get I did this, okay?"

"No. I can't forget. You're disappointed in me." It tore him apart. "I'm working hard. I'm getting stronger. I'm going to be the man I used to be. Someone you can count on. I promise you this. Just don't stop loving me."

"Jonas, you don't understand." She faced him, tears spilling down her cheeks, the sorrow deeper, but the love was there, too.

Relief left him dizzy. He cradled her hands, so small and fragile feeling, and held on so tight, as if he could keep her from changing her mind about him. As if he could keep her right here until he could prove to her he was the man who deserved her. "I've made you unhappy, Dani. I can't stand that. How can I fix this?"

"Oh, my dear husband." Her hands twisted from his.

For one split second he feared she was pulling away from him, that he was losing her, this woman who was his everything. But then she laid her hands, damp with her own tears, against the sides of his face. Her touch sent hope zinging to his soul. Her touch made his fear ease.

"No one told you what today really is, right?"

Her question stumped him. He shook his head. "I did everything your mom and sisters said. If they knew it, then that's what I did. The flowers, the dinner, the balloon ride. The kiss."

"They probably thought you already knew. Today is our anniversary."

"Anniversary?" How had he forgotten that? How had something that important gotten by him? Jonas felt his insides turn cold. Because no amount of pictures and stories could take the place of the richness of those memories.

"We were married eight years ago. About this time, we were probably about ready to land in Seattle, knowing our honeymoon suite was waiting. Our whole life together was waiting. I was so happy to be your wife."

Panic hit him like a speeding truck. She was talking in past tense. Was he going to lose her? His injury had cost him enough—time with his family, precious memories he could never get back. He was not about to let that gunman take his wife from him, too.

"No, Dani." He had been wrong. He had fought so hard for her, but it had been in all the wrong ways. His need to be whole and strong for her, that was for himself, he could see that now. Because he didn't feel lovable being less than the man he was.

But in failing her, he was so much less than he'd ever been. "I didn't remember. I should have. There's no excuse for this. I saw the date in the photo album. I just never thought. I'm sorry."

"I know, Jonas. I just expected too much too soon. Maybe I've been wrong all along." She looked so lost, as lost as he felt.

He had been wrong; but he knew Dani. He knew what she needed now. "Please, give me the chance to make this right. I can make this up to you. I know it. Tell me what to do, and I'll do it."

"No. We had a nice evening. That was enough. It was—" She blinked back the tears from her eyes. "You can't fix this."

"I have to. Dani, don't give up on me. I'm begging you." He had still so much to tackle and to come back from. He was not whole. More anger filled him, anger at the man who had shot him. Pointless anger he had to let go of. "I'll work harder. I will."

"I know, Jonas. I don't doubt you. Never you." She hated how he was hurting. She hated that he'd found her crying over nothing at all—and everything, all at the same time. "I need you. I miss you."

"Dani, I'm right here." So true, that was Jonas. His hands cupping her shoulders, holding on to her, pure unbreakable steel.

"I miss how close we used to be. For a moment tonight in the balloon I thought that it was back. But now, just like that, you turn away from me and it's gone. I missed how it was when you were in love with me." She knew this was where she would say how much she loved him and he would sweetly, wonderfully, perfectly say that he wanted to love her, too. Once, that had been enough. The promise of his love, of regaining their closeness had been enough to keep her going.

But not tonight. Her heart felt too broken, too tired, in too many pieces. Loneliness hurt like an open wound. "I just needed more tonight, Jonas. I need your love. I need to hear the words. I'm so alone without you."

Pain shot across his face. "This is the way you've been feeling? All along?"

"That was my fault, too." She nodded, able to see that now. She hadn't trusted him enough. "From the moment I got your supervisor's call, I was terrified I would lose you. Jonas, you are my center, my strength, my heart on this earth. Until I saw you unconscious on that hospital bed, I didn't realize you were the reason I drew breath. That I am who I am. That I have two amazing children. That today—our anniversary—means more to me because I see this now. I know what true love is. I miss my better half."

"Not your *better* half." He softly kissed the tears from her face. "I did this all wrong, Dani. I should have known how you were feeling. I should have been a better husband to you."

"You are the best husband I could possibly have. The only one I will ever want." How did she make him understand? "You were my best friend, my soul mate, my husband, my life."

"Your everything." He brushed the hair out of her eyes so that he could look into them. "I think I understand. That's what you want back."

She nodded, afraid that he would retreat now. Afraid that he would admit that he was not those things—and maybe never would be.

"Dani, I've tried so hard." Jonas sounded tortured. "I've tried so hard to be what you needed. I've worked so hard to be strong for you."

"I know. This isn't fair to you."

"I thought if I could get back to where I was, that you could love me for who I am. Instead of who I used to be."

"Oh, Jonas. No. I love who you are now." Talk about regrets. She should have been stronger tonight, but she had simply needed him. She still needed her best friend, her husband, to love her. "I've put too much pressure on you. Again."

"No, it's my fault. All mine. I thought I knew you, Dani. What you needed. What you wanted. I've done my best to come back."

Her worst fear was going away from him bit by bit, step by step over time. Heaven knew that happened in marriages. Was it too late for theirs? So much distance had slipped between them. How could she bear to lose him twice?

"But now I see I didn't know you at all." He looked in agony. "What kind of husband doesn't see how much his wife is hurting?"

"You haven't failed me, Jonas. You are much more than the man you used to be. Can't you see that?" Was he going to say he'd done all that he could? That this was all he had to give? She took a shuddering breath. "I'm lonely for you."

"I see that." Tears—pain—filled his eyes. "Have I lost you? Have I messed everything up?"

How could he think this was his fault? Her vision blurred. "Does this mean you still w-want me?"

"Every second of every minute of every day, beautiful." His gaze fastened on hers as if he were seeing far into her heart and into the secret places of her spirit. "I am in love with you. I didn't know how much until now. I think about losing you and my world crashes into pieces. I am nothing without you. It's as if all the light stops and there's just darkness."

"Jonas, that's how I feel, too. I just need your love."

"My heart is the same, and my heart remembers you. I might not love you the way I used to, but I can promise you this. I love you more now than I ever did. And more with every passing minute. My love for you is great and true, and that's something no bullet can stop."

Tears rolled down her cheeks, but no longer from loneliness. His lips found hers with infinite sweetness. His kiss was more than a promise. It was perfection.

She let him draw her into his arms, into the sanctuary of his chest where she belonged. The world felt right again. She savored the sweetness of being close to him, of the distance between them bridged. She soaked up the sound of his heartbeat against her ear and the draw of his breath. How thankful she was for this man. How infinitely thankful.

"Since I'm down on my knees, maybe now is a good time to ask you something." Jonas took her hand, her left hand, where her diamond wedding set sparkled. "Will you do me the honor of becoming my wife?"

"I *am* your wife."

"Yes, but I want a wedding I can remember. One I can share with you." His eyes darkened until there was only the love there, as true as dreams. "Marry me, Dani. Let me promise to love and honor you again, so we both can remember where we've been. Where we will go together."

"Yes. It would be my pleasure to marry you all over again." She kissed her husband so he would know how she felt, how much she adored him and how grateful she was for him. "Thank you, Jonas. For loving me. For not leaving me."

"Never, beautiful." His smile made her soul sigh. "I promise I will love you so hard and true for the rest of my life. I will be right here for you, doing everything I can to be the man you need."

"I know that, Jonas."

"I might get it wrong from time to time, so I'll need you to steer me a little." He winked.

"Gladly." She kissed him, so he would feel how she felt. Suddenly her hopes were sky-high again. Her joy taller than the grandest mountain. She thought of those secrets they'd kept from one another. Her fears. His fears. Anger at the gunman who had shattered their world.

Well, it was whole now. They were going to be all right. She could tell by the way he was looking at her, as if he loved her every shortcoming, every flaw, every strength. Dani swiped the last of the tears from her eyes. Already there was the brightness in her heart that his love had put there.

Yes, she could see he was strong enough to lean on. Just as she was strong enough, too.

Bare feet padded across the linoleum and suddenly little arms wrapped around Danielle's middle. "Mommeee! I want kisses, too!"

"Who is this out of bed?" Jonas growled, gently, teasingly as he grabbed up the little pajama-clad girl and swung her into his arms. "I think she needs to be punished."

Over the top of Madison's curls, he winked at her. Danielle laughed, she felt so happy. "Someone definitely needs a big punishment."

"No, Daddy! Mommy, no!" Madison squealed, wiggling even before Jonas smacked the first kiss on her appled cheek.

"That's one kiss." Danielle snuggled close to leave a smacking kiss on Madison's other cheek. "Two kisses."

"No-ooo!" She giggled.

"Three kisses." Danielle waited while Jonas did the honors, and then she added the next one to Madison's forehead. "Four kisses."

"And a tummy tickle." Jonas's baritone rumbled with laughter as he tickled her.

Maddy giggled with delight. "No! Daddeeee!"

More footsteps sounded behind them. Lucky come to

see what the commotion was about, followed by Tyler, still yawning and sleep tousled.

"Do you know what I think?" Jonas hugged both kids before he climbed to his feet. "We ought to celebrate. Hot chocolate and cookies for everyone."

"Cookies!" Madison agreed with a shout.

"Yeah! Hot chocolate!" Tyler pumped his fist.

Lucky barked, his tail whapped and nearly toppled a chair.

Danielle laughed and felt pure joy sift into her heart. It was like dawn after a stormy night. A sandy, sun-kissed shore at ocean's end.

She let Jonas take her hand and they went into the kitchen together.

Epilogue

Two weeks later

Danielle peered through the windows of her grandmother's house into the sun-swept backyard full of her friends and family. Blooming roses adorned the garden and the arbor, where Jonas waited for her.

Jonas. Her soul filled from simply gazing upon him. In his black tux, he looked like her own personal hero come to life. Which was exactly the truth.

"Oh, you look beautiful, baby." Her mother tapped into the room, lovely as always. "Where are the girls?"

"They ran off to get me the borrowed and blue stuff." Danielle stepped away from the window, but kept it in sight. There was her husband, chatting with their pastor, who had squeezed them into the schedule despite the busy wedding season—and the completely booked church. It hadn't been easy planning a last-minute wedding, but it had been a labor of love.

"This might not be your first wedding, but it's a real one nonetheless. We can't go bucking tradition." Dorrie tapped over to brush at her hair and straighten the veil. "There. You look nervous. Take a deep breath. It's going to be okay."

"I know. It's silly." She glanced at the beveled mirror above Gran's bureau. The woman staring back at her was swathed in the white of her original wedding dress, but she was no longer that young starry-eyed bride from their first wedding photos.

Time and the challenges of life had changed her. There were a few lines on her face—she really wanted to try to ignore seeing those—and she had a more mature look. The love she felt for Jonas had changed, too. Tested by fire, purified in the process, it was stronger. While their bond had been sound before, it was invincible now. The hidden blessing of Jonas's injury.

Heels tapped down the hallway and there was Ava, in her rose-pink bridesmaid dress. "I've got the penny for your shoe. Off with it, Dani."

"Like that's easy in this dress." Danielle couldn't help laughing as she waded through the silk and ruffles for her white satin slippers and was grateful when Dorrie bent to remove the shoe. Danielle stood on one foot, holding on to the chair, while her sister and mom placed the penny and then she wiggled her foot back into the slipper.

"I've got something that's both old and borrowed." Aubrey, newly returned from her honeymoon, swept into the room in her bridesmaid dress holding something small in her hand. "I remembered you wore this in your first wedding. It's Gran's cross."

Emotion burned in her eyes as she gave her sister a kiss

on the cheek and bent down, holding back her hair—Mom grabbed the veil—so Aubrey could place and latch the delicate gold chain.

When she straightened, the beautiful jeweled cross gleamed like love. It had been a wedding gift to Gran from Grandpop, and it was like a sign that this new phase of her marriage would be as blessed as the first eight years had been.

Rebecca rustled into the room, also in her bridesmaid silk, and handed over the bouquet. "I have something blue. I tucked a violet into your roses."

Lauren followed her, the final bridesmaid. "I have something new. It's from your husband."

"Jonas?" That was just like him to think of a gift. She took the box out of Lauren's hand and fingered the quality, beautifully linked chain.

"It's for your old wedding ring," Lauren explained. "He wanted to surprise you with a new one, which is stunning, I might add. This chain is so you can wear your old ring next to your heart."

Yes, that was just like Jonas. As she struggled to get her ring off her finger, she caught sight of him through the window. There went her heart again, soaring up to the sky. Love filled her up so there was no room for anything else.

"It's time to marry your husband." Dorrie took her hand to steady her.

"I can't wait."

With his ring next to her heart, she let her mother and sisters guide her down the stairs—tricky with the dress and train—and into the back doorway.

While she waited for her sisters to precede her down the aisle between the rows and rows of folding chairs, she was joined by two important visitors. Her dad, come to give her away again, and her daughter, dressed up in frothy pink, her maiden of honor.

"Mommy! Look!" Madison twirled until her dress spun out around her and she came to a dizzy stop. "I did it lotza times!"

"I saw." Danielle straightened the girl's pink rhinestone tiara and gave her a smacking kiss on the cheek. "Guess what, princess? It's your turn. Go straight down the aisle to your daddy."

"Okay!" Madison stopped on her way down the aisle to twirl prettily and shout, "Look at me, Mommy."

Then it was her turn. Everyone stood to watch as she stepped out into the sunlight on her dad's arm. The presence of the onlookers, the lull of music from a hired string quartet, the beauty of Gran's backyard and her own nerves faded to nothing. All she saw—all she would ever see—was the handsome man waiting for her at the arbor. His gaze was only for her—his eyes never left hers as she took every step, closing the distance between them.

"I'm s'posed to take your flowers, Mom." Tyler stepped forward in his matching black tux, the most handsome best man in any wedding ever.

"Thank you, sweetie." There had been nothing in her life sweeter than this moment. Tyler took her flowers and gave her a kiss on the cheek. Madison was spinning more circles and Rebecca was gently trying to get her to stop.

Jonas—her treasured Jonas—reached out to take her hand. The moment she laid her fingers on his wide palm, her entire being sighed with joy. Their hands met, and their souls did, too, connected once again, closer than they'd ever been. When he looked upon her with boundless love, she knew the truth. That God had taken a terrible tragedy— an act committed by a desperate man—and turned it into His good. Into a greater love.

"You are my beloved," Jonas whispered in her ear, holding on to her as if he never intended to let her go. "For now and forever."

"As you are mine."

The breeze stirred the leaves in the trees and teased the fragrance from the many roses. The minister began the ceremony, and so they were married with summer sunshine falling over them like grace.

* * * * *

Don't miss Rebecca's story
HER PERFECT MAN
Available from
Love Inspired
August 2008

Dear Reader,

Thank you so much for choosing *Her Wedding Wish*. I hope you enjoyed Danielle's and Jonas's story as much as I did writing it. When their perfect world is shattered after her husband is shot, Danielle does not turn to despair but to her faith and to her love. Love, which is strong enough to see them both through Jonas's recovery—and strong enough to turn tragedy to triumph. We have all had hardship come into our lives at one time or another and often, as in Jonas's case, unfairly. I hope Danielle's and Jonas's struggle through hardship toward love speaks to your life, too.

Wishing you the best of blessings,

Jillian Hart

QUESTIONS FOR DISCUSSION

1. At the beginning of the story, when Jonas and Danielle arrive home after his extended stay in a rehabilitation clinic, what are their primary concerns? What does this say about their characters?

2. What is Jonas's initial behavior toward the children he doesn't remember? What does this reveal about him? About his faith and his values?

3. Danielle has shouldered a lot of burdens over the past year. How has that affected her? What does that reveal about her faith and her values?

4. At the beginning of the story, both Danielle and Jonas believe they can recapture the past. How does this change? How do they both handle this challenge? How do they both face the reality of Jonas never being able to remember?

5. How important is the theme of family in this story?

6. How does Danielle hold on to her hope? Jonas?

7. How important are the themes of compassion and service to others in this story?

8. How is God's leading evident? What do you think God's plan is for Danielle and Jonas?

9. What do you think Danielle and Jonas have learned about anger and forgiveness? About love?

10. How do Danielle and Jonas turn tragedy into triumph?

11. What role does the dog play in the family's healing?

12. How does Danielle's love change Jonas?

REQUEST YOUR FREE BOOKS!

2 FREE INSPIRATIONAL NOVELS
PLUS 2
FREE
MYSTERY GIFTS

Love Inspired®

YES! Please send me 2 FREE Love Inspired® novels and my 2 FREE mystery gifts (gifts are worth about $10). After receiving them, if I don't wish to receive any more books, I can return the shipping statement marked "cancel". If I don't cancel, I will receive 4 brand-new novels every month and be billed just $4.24 per book in the U.S. or $4.74 per book in Canada, plus 25¢ shipping and handling per book and applicable taxes, if any*. That's a savings of over 20% off the cover price! I understand that accepting the 2 free books and gifts places me under no obligation to buy anything. I can always return a shipment and cancel at any time. Even if I never buy another book, the two free books and gifts are mine to keep forever.

113 IDN ERXA 313 IDN ERWX

Name	(PLEASE PRINT)

Address	Apt. #

City	State/Prov.	Zip/Postal Code

Signature (if under 18, a parent or guardian must sign)

Order online at www.LoveInspiredBooks.com

Or mail to Steeple Hill Reader Service:

IN U.S.A.: P.O. Box 1867, Buffalo, NY 14240-1867
IN CANADA: P.O. Box 609, Fort Erie, Ontario L2A 5X3

Not valid to current subscribers of Love Inspired books.

Want to try two free books from another series?
Call 1-800-873-8635 or visit www.morefreebooks.com

* Terms and prices subject to change without notice. N.Y. residents add applicable sales tax. Canadian residents will be charged applicable provincial taxes and GST. This offer is limited to one order per household. All orders subject to approval. Credit or debit balances in a customer's account(s) may be offset by any other outstanding balance owed by or to the customer. Please allow 4 to 6 weeks for delivery. Offer available while quantities last.

Your Privacy: Steeple Hill Books is committed to protecting your privacy. Our Privacy Policy is available online at www.SteepleHill.com or upon request from the Reader Service. From time to time we make our lists of customers available to reputable third parties who may have a product or service of interest to you. If you would prefer we not share your name and address, please check here. ☐

LIREG08

Love Inspired

TITLES AVAILABLE NEXT MONTH

Don't miss these four stories in July

A HEART FOR THE DROPPED STITCHES by Janet Tronstad
Future lawyer Becca Snyder doesn't have time for romance.
She's too focused on her career goals. But seeing Mark Russo's
dedication to his shelter for homeless teens makes her start to
rethink her priorities—and her viewpoint on love.

MISSION: MOTHERHOOD by Marta Perry
Homecoming Heroes
Overnight, Caitlyn Villard becomes a mother to her orphaned
nieces. So Caitlyn trades New York City for the small military
town of Prairie Springs. Adjusting to the town's slow pace isn't
easy. But handsome army chaplain Steve Windham is happy to
show her that home is where the heart is.

HOMECOMING AT HICKORY RIDGE by Dana Corbit
When the black sheep of Hickory Ridge returns home, all eyes
are on him. Only Julia Sims will give Kyle Lancaster the benefit
of the doubt. At first, Kyle worries that he's her new pet project.
Yet Julia's good heart gives him hope for a true second chance.

THE COWBOY TAKES A BRIDE by Debra Clopton
Sugar Rae Lenox can't wait to leave Mule Hollow. And she thinks
the local matchmakers are mighty mistaken for encouraging
the attraction between her and cowboy Ross Denton. He has no
intention of ever leaving town. Is there a future for Sugar Rae and
her cowboy with boots of lead?

LICNM0608